Feel the Force

The inner-city borough of Wallsden was in turmoil, and as usual the trouble seemed to emanate from the Fleetway housing estate. Somebody was going to get killed one of these days, they said.

Only the first death wasn't a Fleetway rioter but a friendly boy from the High Street. It could have passed for an accident if only Detective Chief Inspector Shields had kept his ill-conceived notions to himself.

Policing the sprawling estate meant keeping everything quiet and calm—to initiate a murder investigation among the hostile residents was to poke a wasp's nest with a stick. Somebody could get badly stung.

PATRICIA DONNELLY

Feel the Force

THE CRIME CLUB
An Imprint of HarperCollins *Publishers*

First published in Great Britain in 1993
by The Crime Club, an imprint of
HarperCollins Publishers, 77–85 Fulham Palace Road,
Hammersmith, London W6 8JB

9 8 7 6 5 4 3 2 1

Patricia Donnelly asserts the moral right to be identified
as the author of this work.

A catalogue record for this book is
available from the British Library

ISBN 0 00 232454 7

Photoset in Linotron Baskerville by
Rowland Phototypesetting Ltd
Bury St Edmunds, Suffolk
Printed and bound in Great Britain by
HarperCollins Book Manufacturing, Glasgow

CHAPTER 1

It seemed as if the worst might be over.

People were still running past the red Toyota, but they were running in the opposite direction now, no longer pausing to thump on the roof or kick the tyres. They hadn't the time to start the car rocking, the preliminary to overturning it.

Inspector Bidwell stared out through the crazed glass of her shattered windscreen, trying to make out what was happening further down the street. One of the first vehicles to be overturned was still burning, giving off a thick cloud of acrid smoke. Beyond it she could see others, some on their sides, broken glass everywhere.

The riot had come from nowhere. Bidwell had been on her way back to work when she had run into the High Street end of the trouble, nearly two hours ago. It had been a terrifying experience for her, unable to drive through the solid mass of bodies that filled the narrow street, seeing the knives and baseball bats that, thankfully, they had used not on her but on the car.

She shivered, and pulled the rug around her—she had grabbed it from the back seat to cover her uniform, as she prepared to wait the situation out.

From inside the car the mood of the crowd had been difficult to gauge. The other cars had been empty, Bidwell thought, and when the mob had found her doors locked they had soon given up trying to force them open. Angry they might have been but it seemed that she was not a priority target. The faces that she saw were intent, with a suddenly coalesced, motivating energy.

Jennifer Bidwell was an experienced police officer, an

elegant woman whose reserved beauty had given rise to some comment among her chauvinistic colleagues. She had only been in Wallsden for a few weeks, finding the London suburb an alien and alienating place. She had not had time to get to know many individuals among the community she served. She knew only that they had problems—the present situation a symptom of the worst of them.

She shivered again, one part of her mind noting the fact and putting it down to mild shock.

There had been no question of seeking alternative shelter when the trouble flared. Most of the shops on High Street had been hurriedly closed, though that hadn't saved their windows. As she watched, the face of a child peered round an upstairs curtain in a row of terraced houses nearby, but was quickly pulled away by an unseen adult. To hammer on any of those closed doors demanding help would only attract attention to herself, and would almost certainly lead to grief for any family daring enough to let her in.

In the lull, she remembered her radio, and decided that it was safe to switch it back on.

'. . . I repeat, please acknowledge. Would Inspector Bidwell please call control. Biddy, for Christ's sake . . .' The voice cracked.

She picked up the handset. 'Receiving. Is that you, Len? Sorry, I've been off the air.'

The sigh of relief was audible through the crackle of the instrument. Sergeant Pickering had apparently been worried. 'We've got a bit of a situation going, ma'am. When we couldn't raise you—are you all right?'

'I'm in High Street with a flat tyre and a smashed wind-screen, otherwise fine. I think—' she sat up properly to look out of the windows again—'it seems to be cooling off around this area. But there's a fair bit of damage. Do we know where the centre of the trouble is?'

Sergeant Pickering didn't answer straight away, and

Bidwell could hear another voice speaking to him at the other end. Eventually it was Chief Superintendent Wetherell who answered her, succinctly outlining the progress of the disturbance from the Fleetway housing estate to the industrial area by the river. His confident, slightly pedantic tones implied that everything was under his personal control. 'We've taken charge in most areas, apart from where you are, but there's a bottleneck on Fourmile Road—they've got barricades. You say your car's out of commission?'

'And then some. Look, sir, I can hang on here, it seems to be a backwater now. What we don't want is the cavalry dashing madly to the rescue . . .'

'Point taken. All the same, I'd sooner you were back with us. Just a minute . . .'

Bidwell heard him consulting with someone else, then silence. After a while Sergeant Pickering returned.

'We've just heard from the DCI, he's not far from your position. If you'll stay put he'll come and find you, get you out without any fuss.' An absence of fuss was the hallmark of the Detective Chief Inspector's operations—just knowing he was in the vicinity was enough to lend Jennifer Bidwell a sense of security.

The street was quieter now, though not quite deserted. There was thick smoke rising from behind the block of shops on the far side of the street—Fourmile Road was in that direction. Inspector Bidwell hoped she wasn't in the line of anyone's retreat.

A solitary figure, running, caught her eye. He swerved, crossed the road as if he had only just noticed her car. Like the earlier rioters, he banged on the roof with his fist. But unlike them, when he tried the nearside door it opened. Swinging it wide, he loomed over the Inspector.

'Don't tell me you forgot to lock your doors?' The cultured voice bore no relation to the scruffy appearance.

'I saw you coming,' Bidwell retorted, though she had

only recognized her colleague at the last minute. In skin-tight jeans, a black sweater and a knitted hat in three colours, Detective Chief Inspector Shields looked nothing like his normal suave self.

'You're not hurt?'

'Only my pride—and my pocket. It took me six months to pay off this car.' She began to disentangle herself from the rug. 'What's next?'

'I'm afraid you become my prisoner. Alan's parked the mini just around the corner, but I think we'll play it safe.' Grasping her by the wrist, he pulled her from the car.

She didn't like it, instinctively struggling to free herself.

'Beautiful,' Shields said softly, 'keep that up, we've got company.' Still holding her firmly, he set off jogging towards the intersection.

'Hey, what you got there, man?' They were suddenly confronted by a group of belligerent young blacks. 'That look like some fuzz.'

'This one's mine, brother,' Shields retorted swiftly. 'You go get your own.' He didn't stop moving, pulling Bidwell along with him, and the group stepped aside reluctantly to let them pass. Glancing back as they reached the corner, Inspector Bidwell saw that they were already dispersing.

'Jump in, ma'am.' An unrecognizable Sergeant Crawford, his bright hair hidden by a balaclava, had the door open and the front seat tilted so that Inspector Bidwell could get in the back. They were a well-established team, these two, and the unkind were apt to call Sergeant Crawford a 'model' detective—meaning a small imitation of the real thing. But Bidwell thought no worse of him for his slavish aping of his senior partner. David Shields had about him a sheer professionalism that others besides Alan Crawford could have benefited from.

'Where did you get your outfit, rent a rioter's?' Jennifer Bidwell asked breathlessly. Without being precisely disguised, Shields had managed to make himself look unremarkable, one of the crowd. He was a good-looking man in his late thirties, with dark brown hair and light brown eyes, and was credited by the station gossip with a string of romantic exploits, about which corroborative detail was sadly lacking. 'I wouldn't have recognized either of you,' she said.

'Borrowed the hats from lost property,' Shields answered shortly. 'Are you sure you're all right?' They were on their way back to the station by a roundabout route, keeping well clear of the Fourmile area. 'I'm sorry if I've left fingermarks.'

Bidwell discovered she was rubbing her wrist, absently. 'Oh, no. I'm fine, thanks.' She wanted to say more, but with the relief of her escape came reaction and she found she couldn't trust her voice.

'Pity about your car,' said Shields, 'but it could have been a great deal worse. If you'd been in one of the Pandas . . . Quite a few cars have been overturned.'

'Yes.' She swallowed. 'That was happening in High Street. People just seemed to spring up from nowhere, it's almost as if all this is spontaneous.'

'It may well be,' admitted Shields. 'From what we've seen it's not being directed at all. Just a lot of violence, most of it aimed at shop windows and cars.'

'Any of ours?'

'Hopwood had a narrow escape and Ellis has a broken arm. That's all I've heard. Apparently the other patrols got in safely before things got completely out of hand.'

'That's when we borrowed the mini,' Sergeant Crawford said, as they pulled into the station yard. 'Cops never drive minis.' He let Bidwell out, then got back behind the wheel. 'To the barricades!'

By the time she reached the front office they were out of sight.

*

'So what's the situation now?' Seated behind her own desk with a comforting mug of coffee warming her hands, Inspector Bidwell was being brought up to date with the wider picture.

'Getting back to normal, ma'am, it seems like.' Sergeant Pickering had been pleased to see the Inspector return safely. He thought she looked pale and shaken, but she was obviously trying to put the memory of her ordeal behind her. 'One of the fires burnt itself out but the brigade got through to the others, with our support. The buggers were throwing stones at first but we soon put a stop to that.'

'Any arrests?'

Len Pickering cocked his head on one side, letting the noise down the corridor speak for itself. 'It's only small fry, mind. Them that started it will have made themselves scarce.'

'Do we know who they are?'

'Some of those young bucks from the Fleetway, I shouldn't wonder. They start by demanding their rights and end up going on the rampage. It's happened before.'

Wallsden was a volatile inner-city suburb, and this wasn't the first time tempers had flared. The main target seemed to have been a chain of betting shops, Sergeant Pickering told her, but once the stone-throwing had started the violence had escalated and become indiscriminate.

Inspector Bidwell asked about casualties.

'Geoff Ellis—'

'Had his arm broken. Yes, I know. How did it happen?'

'I've told Hopwood to put in a report. So far most of what he's said is what he's going to do to the yobbos who turned the car over. That's when he finds them.'

'He wasn't in the car at the time?'

'No, his story is that he'd gone into Patel's for a word about their shoplifting problem. More likely it was to get cigarettes—but anyway, he heard the commotion and rushed out just in time to see the car go over. Ellis must have been half asleep, as usual.'

'Anyone else?'

A roll-call of the station staff had revealed a variety of injuries and grievances, among both the uniform branch and the CID. Detective-Constable Mann was suffering from concussion, having been hit by half a brick thrown from one of the balconies on the Fleetway estate. 'Apart from that it's mostly burns and bruises.'

'Right. I'll need to have a note of property damage, our vehicles as well, and I'd like to have a look at Hopwood's report.'

Sergeant Pickering grinned. 'I'd better see how he's getting on.'

Although physically unharmed, Constable Hopwood was complaining loudly, airing his opinions to Constable Wilkes while trying to write his report. He wanted to know why there hadn't been a swifter retaliation ordered—baton charges would have sorted the buggers out.

'Nah, they'll go home quicker this way.' The other man had a bandage on his wrist, having come into close contact with wreckage from a burning building. A long experience in community policing had taught him not to take anything too personally. Today's rioters were tomorrow's clients, with problems he was expected to solve.

'The trouble with you, Tim Wilkes, is you're soft.' Hopwood swore quietly at the typewriter as the keys jammed under his impatient fingers. 'Geoff could've been killed, none of those black buggers cared, made off the minute I appeared.'

'So you don't know who they were?'

'Oh, I know all right, and I'll know them again when I get my hands on them. Leroy Thomas and the Robertson gang,

that's who it'll be. Soon as I've got this stinking paperwork
off my hands I'll sort them out.'

Constable Wilkes grimaced. He was a large man with a
slow, amiable approach to life. His hair was thinning now,
but he kept himself as fit as when he had won prizes for
amateur boxing. Hopwood was nearly twenty years his
junior and he thought the younger man had a lot to learn.

'Leroy's on probation,' he reminded his colleague. 'It's
not likely his gran let him out of the house.'

'So what? If it's not him it'll be one of his crowd. Rotten
sods, all of them.'

'You can't treat the whole community like criminals,
Hoppy, the Super's got the right idea.'

'Super's no better than you—wait till it blows over, he
says. Wetherell? Weathercock, more like.'

Hopwood, had he known it, was voicing a majority view.
Few of that relief were without some evidence of the afternoon's turmoil. They had seen Inspector Bidwell come in,
and heard what had almost happened to her. It was all very
well for the Superintendent to advocate an unprovocative
response to the outrage, but it wasn't his skin that had been
bruised or singed in the process.

Chief Superintendent Wetherell was a pragmatist, seen
by most as the right man for the job in a politically sensitive
area. His natural good humour smoothed his way through
the endless public meetings called to discuss police–community relations. He had the ability to listen to the most
far-fetched notions with a straight face and only a few
favoured associates knew what he really thought of the anti-
racism training that was proposed for his staff.

His appearance always immaculate, Wetherell looked the
part, the embodiment of authority. His undoubted commit-
ment to the job gained him a qualified approval among the
rank and file, especially since it took the form of backing
up his men, regardless of the circumstances. They weren't

so happy about the policies he was trying to implement.

The Chief Superintendent was in his office checking through reports, bringing himself up to date with the situation. He had spent much of the previous hour having a look for himself, ending up at the hospital where three of his men and two from the fire brigade were being treated. Constable Ellis's broken arm was probably the most serious injury, the others being in the nature of cuts, burns and bruises. There had been some anxiety about a case of concussion, but the officer was out of danger.

No serious casualties, no loss of life. Superintendent Wetherell breathed a sigh of relief. It was a vindication of his policies. Damage to property was no doubt extensive but at least none of his people's lives had been lost defending the run-down buildings that lined High Street and Oldwall Road. He was aware of a build-up of tension within himself which was only now beginning to find relief, with the knowledge that once again his conciliatory approach had been successful. Had the violence continued for much longer he would have been forced to call for assistance from outside the division, assistance that would have given the anti-social elements of the borough a more clearly defined target.

He closed the last of the interim reports, and flicked a switch on his intercom. 'Desk Sergeant? Any word from Inspector Shields?'

'Just called in, sir.' The voice was Pickering's, calm and reassuring. 'Fourmile Road's half empty—the DCI says they're slipping off home by handfuls. All we need now's a shower of rain and we'll be able to dismantle the barriers by the time it's dark.'

'And you've got men ready to move?'

'Everybody's in position, sir.'

'Well done, Len.'

'Thank you, sir.'

Wetherell sat back and thought about a cup of coffee, or

something stronger. It was a natural chain of thought from that to the needs of the relief who had stayed on to assist with the emergency—and to the shambles the duty roster would be in. Len Pickering would sort out the details but Wetherell was the man responsible should there be an over-run on the available overtime. It was going to play havoc with the monthly statistics.

The ability to get more and more work from fewer and fewer men, that was what management came down to in today's political climate. Well, he had done his best to contain the affair with the least possible expenditure of manpower. It was at times like this that he was apt to regret his confinement to a supervisory role, and envy DCI Shields his freedom of movement.

The mini was parked inconspicuously in the open doorway of a deserted warehouse. To their left, further down the street, the two CID men could see the police cordon round the fire brigade who were damping down the last of the fires. To their immediate right was the haphazard assortment of oddments that constituted the nearer barricade. Across the street was the smashed window of a retail liquor outlet, and from time to time figures would emerge from behind the barrier to help themselves to another bottle. They seemed to have got tired of standing on top of the heap, hurling defiance at the empty street.

Sergeant Crawford scribbled another name in his notebook. 'Not long now, sir,' he said.

'Just as well.' David Shields tried in vain to stretch his long legs. 'I suppose it had to be a mini? If we don't make a move soon I'm going to be crippled for life.'

Crawford grinned. 'Sorry, sir.' He was not much over medium height himself, compared with Shields's six foot and half an inch. 'Think we should call in the troops?'

Shields nodded. 'Let control know it's time—I'm just

going for a stroll.' He eased himself out of the car and set off casually in the direction of the police reinforcements.

It felt eerie to be out in the open after so much had happened. There was a brooding silence over the deserted street, but it was not the silence of emptiness, rather a sense of someone watching—and waiting. It was almost as if one wrong move could precipitate another outburst of violence. Shields and his sergeant had spent much of the afternoon observing the progress of the riot, noting the systematic looting that had gone on side by side with the almost mindless exuberance. He saw now how Fourmile Road had suffered. Breathing the chill smoke-laden air, he slouched, shoulders forward, until he reached the perimeter of the police cordon.

'That's far enough, sunshine.' A large hand gripped him roughly by the elbow.

Shields pulled his woolly hat off and stood up straight. 'Who's in charge of this unit?'

'Sorry, sir. Didn't recognize you. Inspector Powell's just over there.'

'Thanks.'

'. . . yes, he's here now,' Inspector Powell finished speaking into his radio. 'Well, Mr Shields? I take it we're ready to go?' His voice was taut with thinly disguised impatience. Always a stickler for doing things by the book, Powell was torn between obeying instructions to the letter and openly criticizing the Superintendent's softly-softly approach. 'All right, you men!' He gave the group their orders.

'There's no need to make a fuss,' Shields intervened quietly. 'We don't want to rouse the street all over again.'

'I'm concerned for the safety of my men, sir. Stones can kill as easily as bullets.'

'All I'm saying is–'

'I'd like to stick to the procedure laid down for this kind

of situation, if you don't mind, Chief Inspector. If you have any objections, we can discuss them later.'

It wasn't the time or the place to start an argument, Shields acknowledged, but he didn't want to discuss anything later. He didn't like Powell, who came from Manchester or somewhere equally outlandish, who walked around with a grim, tight smile and an aura of being perpetually right.

Inspector Powell seemed disappointed when nobody stayed to be arrested. The only rioters waiting for them were several inert bodies between the two abandoned barricades. On closer investigation these proved to be neither dead nor injured but merely intoxicated and had to be taken in as drunk and incapable. It was while Powell's men were loading them into the van that the rain started.

It was an appropriate ending to the day. Shields and Crawford made their way back to the station, where Shields thankfully abandoned the mini as well as his unorthodox headgear.

He should have been off duty, long since. But a feeling from the empty street seemed to have stayed with him, a feeling that the night wasn't over. There was the unfinished discussion with Inspector Powell, of course, but since the operation had gone smoothly there was no point in looking for an argument. It was only when he thought about drafting his report that Shields realized how utterly weary he was. Well then, it could wait.

The wet streets were deserted now, the litter and the wreckage waiting for daylight and the cleaning up that would follow. Pressing his shoulders back against the upholstered comfort of his cherished BMW, Shields was thankful that the car had been safe in the Clarence Square yard and not out on the hostile streets.

He drove almost aimlessly, trying to establish in his mind where the violence had started, why it had taken the path it had. Why the public library had been left undamaged while the video shop had been vandalized. Why some of the abandoned vehicles had been left alone and others over-turned.

He stopped in High Street to check Jennifer Bidwell's Toyota. Hopefully insurance would cover the damage but it was always sickening to have your property wrecked in the course of your work. All the same, she had been lucky to escape injury. Shields admired her courage in sticking things out, in not panicking. He admired other things about her as well, though he hadn't yet found an appropriate moment to let her know.

His tired mind strayed from the length of Bidwell's legs to the crisis of his home life—no, not crisis, disaster, he decided. And home life was too dignified a term for the intermittent sharing of premises. A partnership that had been great while they lived apart had rapidly cooled as living together exposed their mutual selfishness. Perhaps it was time he admitted that his career came first, just as hers did.

Shields glanced at his watch as he re-started the car. Kelly would be home soon, perhaps they could talk tonight, find an amiable solution to their difficulties. One part of his mind dwelt on the amiable idea—if they decided to part friends perhaps they could celebrate in the time-honoured way.

He drove on past a burnt-out wreck, beyond which lay an overturned Renault. It was a nice car, one of the latest models, in a fashionable metallic grey. It hurt to see it mindlessly vandalized. He had passed the pathetic sight, but something glimpsed in his rear-view mirror made him slow down. He reversed as far as the Renault and got out of his car.

Walking slowly around the overturned vehicle, Shields cast his mind back to when he had last seen it, when he had rescued Jennifer Bidwell. Surely it had been lying on its side then? Now it was right over on its back, pathetic as a dead tortoise.

There was something else.

Shields grabbed a torch from his own car, then crouched down on the pavement to peer through the broken glass where the driver's window had been. The shadowed bulk beyond could have been almost anything but the brown flaccid shape reflecting the light was certainly a human hand.

The driver was still in the car.

CHAPTER 2

Mrs Charles pushed the front door closed behind her with a sense of relief. Yesterday's disturbance had settled down, but there was evidence of mischief on the quiet street still. Had it been only for herself, she wouldn't have bothered shopping, but she liked Willis to get a proper meal to start the day.

She picked up the plastic bag, climbing the narrow flight of stairs to their first-floor flat. Most of Willis's mates lived on the Fleetway estate, she supposed that was where he was now, but she still struggled to maintain the tiny flat that she and her late husband had first managed to rent nearly twenty years ago. It had been over the grocer's then, now the property was an op-shop, a failing half-hearted one at that. She had seen the neighbourhood come down and down over the years.

She had bought a bit of bacon, planning to fry bread with it—an extravagance, but she knew it would reassure her son, make him feel that things couldn't be that bad. They could, of course, and were. Since she'd lost her cleaning job Mrs Charles ate little herself, fighting only to keep the illusion of a home together so that the boy wouldn't be ashamed to come back to it. He'd promised to be home early last night, but it made sense for him to have stayed where he was and off the streets. That was where the trouble was.

As she turned down the gas under the frying-pan, she heard the street door pushed open, and heavy footsteps on the stairs. She waited for the caller to identify himself in some way—naturally trusting, it had taken a lifetime in this neighbourhood to train her in caution.

'Mrs Charles?' The voice of authority. 'Can we come in, please? It's the police, from Clarence Square. We'd like to have a word with you.'

She clutched at her chest, frightened by the accelerated beat. It had long been her dread that the unexpected visit from the police which happened to so many mothers in Wallsden would eventually happen to her. Willis must have gone out last night after all. She flung open the door and stared at them, the young, ridiculously young, woman and the older man. Smart in their uniforms but tired-looking.

'You come on in. That Willis, he a good boy, he's friends lead him into this trouble.'

They didn't specify the trouble. 'This is WPC Mason— I'm Constable Wilkes. Sorry to disturb your breakfast.'

'That cooking for the boy.' She crossed to the stove and switched it off. 'You better tell me what he done.'

They didn't seem to be in any hurry. The man Wilkes looked around, then asked if they could make her a cup of tea. The policewoman was leading her to a chair and urging her to sit down. Again she was conscious of her heart, and a breathlessness, as if she had just run up the stairs—as if she ever did that nowadays.

'That trouble on the streets,' she began, 'I know my Willis didn't do nothing bad. But maybe he out watching all them bad things happen.' Mrs Charles didn't have much to do with the police, was inclined to disbelieve the tales that Willis had brought home in the past. These people looked like good people, with a caring look about their white faces.

Then they began to talk to her.

Although she could hear the words quite clearly, she found they made no sort of sense. High Street and a Renault car that had been overturned. No, there was no way Willis would do anything bad like that. Then she tried to hit out at the words, because it wasn't possible that they could be saying what they were.

'God, Tim, I hope I never have to go through that again.'

It was sheer breathlessness that had finally made Mrs Charles stop screaming. Anita Mason had fussed over her, trying to make her drink the tea she had brewed, while Wilkes located a neighbour who could spare the time to sit with her.

'It's all part of the job.' Wilkes felt shaken himself, but had no intention of showing it. 'Not that it ever gets any easier.'

They had tried to explain the circumstances to Mrs Charles, that in a way it had been an almost accidental death, that in the heat of the moment whoever overturned the car had not given any thought to its occupant. 'But we'll find out who did it, Mrs Charles, you can be sure they'll be punished,' Wilkes had told her. He might as well have saved his breath.

'What's she going to do now?'

Wilkes shook his head tiredly. A middle-aged widow living for her one son, there wasn't much left for her to do. He had seen it all before, and knew he should try to stop WPC Mason from getting emotionally involved. 'Somebody's bound to look after her, there may be other family. Perhaps Billie Morgan can do something. I don't know.' After radioing in to control they continued walking their beat in silence. Back to the old routine.

Reluctantly, the community was pulling itself together. Street cleaners were busy. The young were conspicuous by their absence.

In High Street, the area where the grey Renault had been overturned was still cordoned off, though the car had been towed away for forensic examination. Willis Charles, who had been identified by the library card in his pocket, was assumed to have died of a broken neck. As Wilkes had told WPC Mason, in the circumstances the post-mortem was a formality.

At Clarence Square, the station was almost overwhelmed with processing those careless enough to get themselves nicked the night before. Happily the media had only recently picked up on the affair and since there was no opportunity to film police wielding batons or assaulting civilians, they were inclined to play it down. There were reporters present, waiting for Chief Superintendent Wetherell to make one of his familiar bland statements, but hardly enough of them to inconvenience the due processes of the law.

Billie Morgan was already there, in her capacity as a social worker as well as representing the residents of the Fleetway estate where she also lived. The atmosphere was different from the previous evening, when the detainees had been on a natural high from defying authority. Now, after a night in custody, many were sullen and rather frightened by the rumour of sudden death.

'Well now, if it isn't Miz Morgan.' Jack Vernon came up behind Billie suddenly, standing unnecessarily close. 'Come to see how many of your clients we'll be putting away?'

'I thought it was just a matter of taking their names and sending them home,' she answered coldly. She wished Inspector Shields were here—she had met DC Vernon before and she didn't like him. It was typical of the man that when she turned round to face him, and to get her bottom out of range of his over-free hands, he continued to crowd her.

Snooty bitch, he was thinking to himself. Yesterday had been hard on all of them, and though Vernon had not reported sick he had his share of minor injuries. He was tired, particularly he was tired of black women telling him how to do his job. Vernon had only one use for a woman like Billie Morgan. He had intimated as much, once, and didn't appreciate her response.

'They can go home when they've told us just what they've been up to. Perhaps.' Vernon's eyes left Billie's face and focused instead on the T-shirt she was wearing under her denim jacket. Black on white, the slogan it bore merely supported the local football team, but Vernon seemed to be having difficulty spelling it out. With one finger he pushed the jacket back from her left breast.

'Keep your hands to yourself!'

'Not elegant enough for you, are they,' he sneered. 'Keeping yourself for Mister Right? Or should I say—?'

'I didn't come here to argue with you,' she interrupted fiercely. 'I came to see if I could help these people.'

'Yes? Then you'll have your work cut out!'

'What d'you mean?'

'Somebody's gone too far this time. I don't suppose you were here last night after the guv'nor found that dead 'un? Because this time your little friends aren't going to be sent home with a slapped wrist, they're going to be looking at a life sentence.'

'It's an open and shut job,' Jack Vernon had told DS Crawford earlier, in the CID room. 'Just means we can get those black buggers from Fleetway a nice long stretch. Rioting can be made to look political by some of the loonie brigade, but causing death is something else again.'

'How many have we picked up so far?' Crawford said, rifling through the sheets on Vernon's desk.

'D'you mind?' Paperwork was the bane of Vernon's life. 'Look, mate, if you're so keen you can finish sorting this lot!'

Alan Crawford laughed. Young he might be, but he wasn't stupid. 'No, thanks. I've got figures of my own overdue.'

'Those thefts on the Fleetway? You can forget that lot till the Willis Charles killing is sorted out. Hang about a bit . . .' Vernon rechecked the file he had just put down.

'What is it?'

'This Robertson, we've had him before, some of his gang anyway. Isn't he some sort of connection with Councillor Kingston? I might just go down and have a word with Mr Robertson.'

'The guv'nor should be in soon.' Said offhand, it was nevertheless a warning, but Jack Vernon dismissed it. He didn't need anybody telling him what to do.

The holding cells which had been crowded the night before had been cleared a little, by a variety of means. Some of the juveniles had been returned to their parents with a caution, others had been bailed at the local magistrates court. Trace Robertson had finally been left with the cell to himself, and a lot to think about.

DC Vernon had found Billie Morgan waiting—presumably for Shields—and had enjoyed making her jump.

'Mrs Robertson asked me to—' Billie Morgan began, but Vernon interrupted her.

'Worried, is she? Well, you can tell her from me she's got good reason to be. Still, if you want to hang around you can see him when I've finished with him—might be glad of somebody to hold his hand. Though I must say—' Vernon looked her over in a way that made Billie's blood boil– 'I wouldn't't've picked him as your type. Bit on the young side, even for you.' He hesitated over the word young, as if it wasn't exactly what he meant. 'Now, why don't you get a nice cup of tea while you're waiting?'

'You, you patronizing pig!' Billie spat out. 'I've a right to see—'

'You're almost beautiful when you're angry, you know that?' There was a note of genuine wonder in his voice. 'Perhaps that's what the DCI sees in you, though I don't expect you call him names, do you?' She was staring at him as if puzzled and Vernon laughed shortly. 'Don't come the innocent with me, darling. I know all about those late night community conferences at your flat—or in your bedroom!'

Billie checked her first angry retort, then became aware that her silence would appear a guilty one. Vernon's expression said as much. In point of fact she and Shields were not lovers—yet. But they were warm friends, and Billie knew David Shields well enough to know that he would back off at the first hint of a scandal. In so far as Jack Vernon was a danger, he would have to be placated. She made a brief denial of his allegation, and no further demands.

Detective-Constable Vernon watched her walk away, a satisfied grin on his face. He wouldn't have minded a bit of that himself, he thought, admiring the back view of the way she filled out her jeans.

Robertson got up as the CID man entered his cell. 'Can I go home now?' In spite of what Vernon had said, he was not as young as some of the other rioters, and he was aware that he would be regarded as the ringleader. Tall and good-looking, he had joined in the violence with a will, not bothering to efface himself. It had been sheer bad luck that his group had been picked up, stopping to loot an electronics shop on their way home. It hadn't been part of the plan, and his uncle was going to be very angry.

DC Vernon smiled. It wasn't a nice smile, more an indication of what might be to come. 'Of course you can go home, Trace,' he said. 'Just as soon as you've told us what we want to know.'

The prisoner sat down. 'I don't know nothing.'

Vernon smiled again. 'I believe you,' he said, with patent sincerity. 'You're twenty-two, you've had eleven years' education at the taxpayers' expense, you've never done an honest day's work in your life and you're pig ignorant.

"Ignorant" is a big word meaning you don't know nothing,' he explained.

'I want my brief.'

The sudden shout of laughter sounded genuine. 'You people,' chuckled Vernon, 'you've got this marvellous sense of humour, haven't you? Natural comics. Still—' he got down to business—'much as I'd like to stay and listen to some more of your jokes, I'm afraid I've got work to do. My boss—' he glanced at his watch—'being one of the leisured classes, might be dragging himself to the station soon, seeing it's nearly dinner-time. I want to keep him sweet, just like you've got to keep me sweet. All it takes is a couple of names.'

Shields woke up with a bad taste in his mouth.

Disoriented by the daylight flooding his room, he took a moment to remember why he had overslept. Raising himself on one elbow he glanced at the radio-alarm beside his bed and calculated that he had had nearly four hours' sleep. Well, that would have to be enough.

Kelly had already gone, the tidied covers on her side of the bed reminding him of the increasing distance between them. She had been half awake when he finally crawled into bed, but he had been too exhausted to do anything about it. That he had fallen asleep despite her snuggling up to him would be taken, he knew, as a direct rejection. It was not going to be a nice day.

A shower helped, and a mug of strong coffee, but he wasn't in the mood for breakfast. Reflecting that it was a pity he had given up smoking, his thoughts returned to the activities of the night, and, as a consequence, what the day would hold.

By now the uniforms would have broken the news to the young man's family. Shields hoped they'd done it carefully. Perhaps he should have done it himself, but it had been two in the morning when the tentative identification had been made.

Willis Charles. Probably no more than nineteen and possibly younger. He had been dressed in the uniform of the area, jeans and a T-shirt, without, for once, the ubiquitous knitted hat. There should have been a sweater, or a jacket of some sort, it had not been a warm evening even before the rain set in. No wallet, nothing in his pockets but a disreputable handkerchief and a plastic card—they had thought at first it was a credit card but closer investigation revealed the logo of the Wallsden Public Library.

The car bore no relation to the body found in it—almost brand new and obviously well cared for. The easy answer was that Charles had been joyriding when disaster met him, but Shields distrusted easy answers. Fingerprints, ownership papers and above all a meticulous post-mortem examination—all these would be needed before Shields began to put any trust in the obvious.

The streets were quiet. He hoped it was the normal after-math and not a sign that something worse was brewing. He found the station busier than usual, but that was natural in the circumstances.

'Good morning, Alan. Any developments?'

'Nothing unexpected, sir.' Detective-Sergeant Crawford was the only occupant of the CID room. 'Tim Wilkes said the boy's mother was very upset, but that's hardly sur-prising.'

'Was she used to him getting into trouble?'

'Apparently not. CRO have nothing on him either. Must have been his first time.'

'Anything else?'

Sergeant Crawford hesitated.

'Jack Vernon's had a word with one of the overnighters, Trace Robertson. He claims young Charles was a runner for Iggy Sparrow. Says he—'

'And I suppose Jack let slip that Charles is dead?'

Crawford pulled a face. 'I hadn't thought of that,' he admitted. Vernon had been cock-a-hoop about getting even one name out of the taciturn Robertson and had gone out to talk to the fence in question. 'Do we follow it up?'

'Search the Charles home? Yes, we'll have to, in any case. But not just yet.' There were other things to be done, routine reports to be examined. They would need to talk to the owner of the overturned car as well, check if anyone had reported it missing. 'I must see Jennie Bidwell.'

Inspector Bidwell was in her office, for once, and looked up with a smile as the DCI entered. 'I heard what happened after I'd gone,' she said. 'Did you get any sleep at all?'

'Some. Not enough,' he added, swallowing a yawn. 'You've had someone round to tell the mother?'

She nodded gravely. 'I sent Mason with Tim Wilkes— a bad experience, I'm afraid, for both of them.'

'Mrs Charles didn't know her son was a tearaway?' Shields sounded doubtful.

'Absolutely not. But she's living on next to nothing, try-ing to feed the boy properly and stay respectable herself. In a cramped flat with no amenities.'

'In that case it won't take us long to turn it over.'

Jennifer Bidwell frowned. It was an insensitive remark, and unlike Shields. One of the things that attracted her to him, apart from his obvious good looks, was the occasional glimpse of a caring person underneath the undoubted efficiency. 'I can get hold of Tim to go along with your people, if you like—'

'Don't bother. I want a word with Mrs Charles on my own account. The word is that the boy was working for Iggy.'

That would explain it. Iggy Sparrow had been a thorn in the side of CID for a long time. Indisputably a villain, his activities seemed beyond reach of proof positive, and each time he was picked up his ultimate release simply underlined their powerlessness.

Just then the phone rang.

'Yes? Yes, sir, he's here.' Inspector Bidwell handed the receiver to Shields. 'The Chief Superintendent wants a word,' she said, watching his reaction. Shields had a way of schooling his expression to one of polite impassivity when speaking to his superiors.

'Right away, sir,' he said as he put the phone down.

'What is it?' Bidwell asked quietly. 'You look unhappy about something.'

Shields hesitated. 'High Street. I've read your report, you saw a car go over, didn't you?'

She nodded. 'I saw more than one, but if you mean the Renault, yes. I saw it overturned.'

'That's what I thought.'

The phone rang again, and Shields left while she was dealing with the minor emergency.

'Ah, David.' Chief Superintendent Wetherell was obviously waiting for Shields. 'Just wanted a quick word before the press conference. Any good news I can make public?'

'On the killing? We're still waiting for the post-mortem. I don't want to say too much because it's beginning to look like a set-up.'

'A what? What d'you mean?'

'There's a possibility Willis Charles wasn't in the car when it was overturned—'

'I can't tell the press that!'

'No, sir. We haven't any proof in any case—'

'Just a moment. Sit down, David, this is important.' Superintendent Wetherell leaned forward, his hands clasped, his voice taking on the confidential overtones that made him so successful a public speaker. 'You know this district as well as anyone here, and I've every confidence in you. You know how easy it is to stir up the community council people. The press are always looking at us, pointing the finger at our, er, community relations.' Wetherell never used the word race if he could possibly avoid it.

'What we have here is an unfortunate incident, a death caused in the heat of mindless violence. Tragic, of course, but I'm sure we are going to be able to target the group of young people involved, and they will be charged. With manslaughter, David.' After a pause to let that sink in, Wetherell added, 'There's no room for any insinuations about premeditated murder. That is what you're hinting at?'

'Inspector Bidwell and I both saw that car on its side and empty, three or four hours before I found Charles.'

'I'm afraid you're not listening to me.'

Oh, I'm listening all right, thought Shields, even if I don't believe my ears. 'Are you telling me to drop this inquiry?'

'Of course not! Good heavens, Shields, this is a sudden death! Of course, we have to know who is responsible, that is, whose actions were the cause of this unfortunate affair. All I'm saying, and I see I must spell it out more clearly, all I'm saying is that I don't want anything to aggravate the present tension. Nor do I want the press to think we are in the business of persecuting the young, er, the younger members of the community.' The Chief Superintendent didn't like using the word black either.

CHAPTER 3

God, the man was fat.

Detective-Constable Vernon listened to the mealy-mouthed reassurances that Iggy Sparrow uttered, disinclined to believe a word.

'Now, would I lie to you?' Sparrow spread his pudgy hands. 'Check with your records, if you wish. Have I ever been convicted of any wrongdoing?'

Of course not, he was too slick for that.

'On the contrary, I think you'll find, er, are you sure you wouldn't like one?' He was offering Vernon a chocolate from a half-empty box. 'No?' He devoted some time to choosing one for himself, popping it into his small round mouth. He sat in, or rather, overflowed, an armchair in the corner of the room. Vernon was forcibly reminded of a spider in the corner of a web.

The flat was on the ground floor of one of the central Fleetway blocks. It had been designed as a family unit but Iggy Sparrow lived alone, ostensibly—there were always one or two minders in the background such as the tough-looking character who had let Vernon in.

'On the contrary. I've gone out of my way to assist the police with their inquiries.' He had been chewing vigorously on a caramel and a thin trail of chocolate oozed from the corner of his mouth. Vernon felt sick.

'According to our information—' he began.

'Ah, yes. The anonymous informer. Or was it one of those hoons picked up for disorderly behaviour, trying to save his poor hide? What was the name again?'

'Willis Charles.'

'So. He lives on the estate?'

'He's dead, Mr Sparrow. But somebody thought he might have worked for you.'

The fat man was staring at him, his eyes hard and brutal, a strange contrast to the softly rounded throat and chin. 'Was he by any chance black?' There was a hint of outrage in the quiet tones. 'Are you suggesting that I would employ such a man? In times like these when my own countrymen are out of work by the thousand?'

Oh, shit. Jack Vernon listened impatiently to the rising diatribe, knowing that Sparrow could go on in this vein for hours.

'At least we know who owned the car.' Detective-Sergeant Crawford was still trying to make conversation, on their way back from visiting Mrs Charles. 'We might get something useful from him.' Shields grunted what might have been an assent. He was aware of Alan's attempts to cheer him up, but he didn't appreciate them.

The search of Willis Charles's meagre belongings had yielded nothing. The poky little bedroom with its bunk bed and chest of drawers was soon searched, as were the cheap clothes hanging in a curtained alcove. The whole flat was barely the size of a decent room, thought Shields. It would almost have been abnormal for the boy to grow up honest in such circumstances, but they would have to look elsewhere for the evidence. Mrs Charles had mentioned that her son had had friends on the Fleetway estate, and Crawford had conscientiously written down the half-dozen first names that were all she could remember. They would go on to visit them later, but first came the appointment with the man who owned the Renault.

'It should be somewhere round here,' Crawford murmured to himself, having given up trying to get a response from Shields. He wondered what was wrong, but knew better than to ask. If Shields had been moved by the woman's distress he would see it as a weakness on his own part. Alan Crawford remembered the one time when he had blundered into some personal preoccupation of the Chief Inspector's and got his head bitten off for his pains.

They had left the respectable poverty of the High Street area, bypassed the sprawl of the housing estate and reached the riverside. Here on the edge of the industrial wasteland were the solid, small villas that had originally housed the factory managers and owners.

'River Lane. That's it.'

Part of a terrace block which had been comprehensively restored, No. 18 had carriage lamps beside the porch and a polished brass knocker on the green-painted door. There was also a doorbell, and Shields pressed this firmly.

To their surprise, Horace Clarke came to the door himself. He was large and prosperous-looking, with a handlebar moustache and a jolly manner that reminded Shields forcibly of a used-car salesman.

'You've come about the Renault, I suppose?' His voice was high and somewhat plaintive, out of character with his appearance. 'Come in, come in.' As he showed them into an elegant drawing-room he glanced carelessly at the ID that Sergeant Crawford offered, plainly uninterested.

'Can I get you a drink? No? You don't mind if I . . . ?' Clarke helped himself from one of the bottles displayed on an antique-style sideboard.

'Where were you yesterday, sir, during the period of the rioting?'

'In the city, of course.' He glanced at his watch. 'I should be there now, but for that call from your people.'

'Where do you work?'

Clarke named a prestigious import firm with offices near Victoria. 'I'm a rep, my work takes me to the continent from time to time, but just now there's a panic at Head Office. I'm by way of being a trouble-shooter,' he explained.

'When did you last use your car?' Shields had found himself a straight chair, not liking the soft leather of the fashionable three-piece suite.

'At the weekend. Ran down to Brighton. Visiting friends.' Clarke took no exception to the questioning, giving the impression of a man who only wanted to be helpful. 'You see, I never drive in town, well, it's not worth it. It's not just the traffic it's all the hassle of parking on top of it. Then there's the risk of some bastard taking it into his head to vandalize the paintwork. No, that Renault cost me a month's salary, I like to think of it being safe and sound.' He thought about it. 'At least, I *did*.'

'And you missed it, when?'

Clarke stared at the Sergeant. 'I didn't. It was your people who let me know what had happened. They said it was a write-off!'

'Where do you normally keep the car, parked outside?' It was a quiet street, the car should have been safe enough.

'No, no. There's a block of lock-up garages at the end of the lane. I told you I kept it safe. D'you want to have a look?' He was looking puzzled. 'I say, d'you mind telling me what all this is really about? I mean, detectives don't usually worry about car conversion, do they?'

It was Shields who answered him.

'I take it you know that your car was found overturned by rioters in Wallsden High Street?'

'Yes.'

'And that's all you know?'

'What else is there?'

'The police found the dead body of a young man in the driver's seat. We'd like to know how it got there.'

They were back in Crawford's car, heading for the Fleetway estate. The search of the lock-up garage had yielded little in the way of clues—the padlock securing the door had been forced and then hung back, secure enough to the casual glance.

More interesting had been Clarke's reaction to Shields's statement. Clearly shocked by the reported death, he had seemed to collapse inside, losing all his beautiful self-possession. They had left behind them the shell of the man who had welcomed them into his home.

'What did you think of that, Alan?'

'Clarke, you mean? He seemed to fall to pieces, didn't he? It's almost as if . . .' Sergeant Crawford hesitated.

'As if he might have known who took the car?'

'Yes. But not what they wanted it for.' Crawford was silent, thinking how far-fetched it sounded. 'You want me to find out who he knows, who he might be involved with?'

It was a technique they had used before, following up circles of acquaintance until somewhere the circles overlapped. 'Anyway, we're here. Who do you want to see first?'

'We'd better drop in on Noah, get a bit of background.'

Noah Franklyn was the recently appointed youth worker. Shields liked what they had seen of him so far, in that he was politely cooperative with authority. Yet he had still managed to gain the confidence of the residents of the sprawling estate. The Fleetway was one of the better-planned housing estates in that there was at least vehicle access to each of the massive central blocks. There had been a time when it was unsafe to leave a car unattended —no doubt it would be so again, but the present fashion in crime was for burglary. Provided a car was neither new nor had expensive extras, it would probably remain untouched. There was even parking space beside the one-storey flat-roofed building that was their destination.

Officially Noah Franklyn was there to co-ordinate services to the younger members of the self-sufficient community, most of whom, like him, were black. But he had quickly made friends among the older, retired residents.

One of them, Ron Purvis, was seated with him in the bleak hall that served the estate as community centre.

There was a game of basketball in progress, but it seemed a desultory sort of affair. Most of the players were in the younger age bracket, school-leavers or drop-outs. As the two CID men entered, concentration lapsed, the ball rebounding from a youngster who had turned to watch them.

'Come on, Jed.' Noah walked over to restart the game. 'You can do better than that!'

''Afternoon, Mr Shields.' Ron Purvis was a small rotund man, but hard like a rubber ball, his roundness accentuated by his almost bare scalp. 'You pick your moments, dontcher?'

'What do you mean?' Shields stood beside him in the corner of the hall. Sergeant Crawford had wandered across to stand beside Noah Franklyn as he tried to ginger up the players.

'I mean as how the Old Bill in't exactly welcome round the estate. Persons non grater as you might say.'

Shields was surprised at that. He thought the rioters had been dealt with almost leniently, considering the provocation.

'So what's the gossip?'

'There's a kid dead, isn't there? Somebody's going to get fitted up for that!'

'Did you know him? Personally, I mean.'

'He come round here a lot. Friendly little sod, helped Noah out and all.'

'So you'll be able to tell us who his friends were?'

Shield's tone was friendly, relaxed. There was silence as they watched the less than inspiring game. Shields was pleased to note that Sergeant Crawford and Noah seemed to be deep in conversation.

'Well, Ron?'

'Mr Shields. It wouldn't be that you're mixing me up with somebody else? Somebody you slips money to for information?'

Shields managed to look hurt at the suggestion, saying that such an idea never occurred to him. 'No, I was just relying on your sense of community. After all, you must know most of what's going on. But of course, we wouldn't want you to be out of pocket . . .'

'I can tell you one thing for free.'

'And that is . . . ?'

'There's one bloke knows everythink as goes on round the estate. By now he'll know you lot are noseying round here—next thing'll be you're going to hear how me or Noah's been done over.' Purvis got to his feet. 'You got your job to do, I knows that. But half them b-basketballers'll be running round to Spadger's place the minute they get out of here.'

Iggy Sparrow. Shields thought about that. 'Does he keep a watch on your flat as well?'

'Nothink so obvious. I'd better be off now, let you have a word with Noah. I generally put the kettle on about now, say, half an hour or so.'

Shields nodded.

Before long, Noah dismissed the Sergeant and turned his full concentration on the game. When they were outside, Shields asked what, if anything, Crawford had learned.

'He's given me the names we wanted.'

'And addresses?'

'Yes, but . . .'

'I know, don't go straight from him to them—no wonder he was looking at the size of my feet!' As they walked back to the car, Shields was taking stock of the featureless blocks of flats that formed most of the Fleetway estate. There was a quietness about it, less outward activity than usual, but a sense that all the windows were occupied with watchers.

It would look suspicious if they drove away after seeing just Noah.

'We'll start with Victor House,' Shields decided. Ron Purvis lived on the ground floor, and should have the kettle on by now.

'I was hoping you'd've thought better of it,' Ron complained as he opened the door to them.

Nevertheless, he was helpful.

Purvis's flat was on a more generous scale than Mrs Charles's place, made comfortable by homemade furniture, shelves and cupboards. Ron Purvis was obviously something of a handyman. He busied about clearing teacups and a plate of biscuit crumbs off a marquetry coffee table. Shields asked about his visitors.

'Nah. Only my mate Dick, you know him, dontcher? Old fool. Wants to have a whip-round for Willie's mum, but what's the point? It's not as if they lived on the estate. We've got our own to look to first. He's one of them do-gooders, that's his trouble—still, never mind him. It's Willie you've come about, isn't it?'

He knew less about Willis Charles's friends than about the boy himself, he told them. 'You might get somethink from Trace Robertson, mind. He kept a bit of an eye on young Willie.'

'Was he one of Robertson's gang?'

'Nothink like that. More of a mascot. Like I said, he were friendly with everybody, white as well as black, into everythink as well.'

'We heard he was working for Iggy Sparrow?' Crawford suggested quietly.

Ron Purvis rubbed his ear and pulled a face.

'I wouldn't have put it like that,' he said. He thought for a while. 'Willis Charles—I knew his dad in the old days, at Croydon.' Seeing that this meant nothing to the two CID men, he explained. 'RAF Croydon. Before either of you two was ever thought of, me and Willard Charles fought the Battle of Britain!' His face took on a defensive expression. 'Leastways, we kept the planes in the air for them.' He explained that Willis's dad had always said that he would return to Britain if he ever got the chance. 'Then I bumped into him down the market, years after, that was. He'd just married Bette, she was a real looker in them days, and had a kiddie on the way. That was Willie. So I've known him all his life, you might say.'

'What happened to his father? Did he leave them?'

'Not in the way you mean. Got himself killed nearly ten years ago. That would have been before your time and all.'

There was something contemptuous about the statement, something bitter.

Ten years ago Shields had been a detective-sergeant in his native St Albans, highly ambitious and desperate to get his transfer to the Met.

'What happened?' Shields asked again.

'There was a break-in, wasn't there? They was living over the grocer's in High Street, and Will was in the shop chatting with old Mr Singh. Half a dozen skinheads broke in to trash the place. Died of head injuries and the police never nailed any of the bastards.'

He was silent with his thoughts for a while, before Shields reluctantly interrupted to ask about the connection with Sparrow.

'Spadger collects information, that's what he does. Willie didn't deal with him direct but he got on all right with my friend Mr Shipley. He's a proper gent, lives across the hallway from me. Used to be a lawyer, but he's retired now. He might talk to you.'

'What d'you mean, he might?' Alan Crawford asked.

'Told you, he's a lawyer.' Purvis grinned lopsidedly. 'Charges for his time, doesn't he?'

It looked like a good lead, but Mr Shipley proved to be

unavailable. Standing outside his deserted flat, Shields got
an uncomfortable feeling. It worsened as other doors turned
out to be locked against them, even though their occupants
were probably at home.

House to house inquiries were hardly their responsibility,
but in the aftermath of the disturbance Superintendent
Wetherell would be reluctant to offer the provocation of
sending uniforms on to the estate. Shields and his sergeant
made several calls at random before stopping at one of the
addresses supplied by Noah Franklyn.

They were in luck. Though not exactly welcome, they
were let into the flat by a young woman, Cal Frazer, who
had been named as a friend of Willis Charles. Shields
thought she had been crying.

'Where were you last night, Miss Frazer?' Sergeant
Crawford asked after she had shown them into the front
room.

'I didn't do nothing,' she replied sullenly.

'We still need to know where you were, who you were
with. Willis Charles, for instance?'

She shook her head.

'I didn't see Willis again, after we'd been to look at the
fun. The crowds,' she explained.

'What time would that have been?'

'Can I sit down?'

'Yes, I'm sorry.' Superintendent Shields came back from
the window where he had been looking out at the general
view of the estate. They were on the fifth floor of Nelson
House by then. He was almost sure there were more young
people about than there had been.

'Did Willis Charles come back here with you?' Crawford
asked her again.

'No. He had to see the man. I wanted to come back
before six o'clock—because of my old lady. She gets in from

work at six.' Perhaps out of habit Cal glanced at the clock on the mantelpiece.

Shields asked her what man Willis meant, but Cal said she didn't know.

'Could it have been Mr Shipley?' Shields hazarded a guess. It must have been a good guess because the girl looked sick. 'Well?'

'I don't know nothing about that,' she whispered.

Shields left it for the moment, instead asking again what time she had parted from her friend.

'I can't be sure.' She bit nervously at her lower lip. 'I think it might have been about half past four, or quarter to five—that's at the latest. It could have been earlier.'

'And where, exactly?'

'Corner of Oldwall, just past the traffic lights. I had a hell of a job getting through the crowd, but Willis stayed the other side. I don't know where he went after.'

'What did you make of her, Alan?' Shields asked as they climbed the stairs to the next level. They still had company, he noted. The growing crowd of youths who had been following them at a discreet distance was hovering at the far end of the walkway.

They had been unable to get anything more out of Cal Frazer—she was obviously frightened and close to tears. But she stuck to the story she had told them.

'It doesn't make sense—if Charles was on his way to see Shipley, surely he would have walked back to the Fleetway with her?'

'It's hard to know.' Shields had the feeling that Shipley might be quite important to the case.

'We could take Frazer in for questioning,' Crawford persisted, but Shields shook his head. In other circumstances perhaps, but now wasn't the time for two white policemen

to take a black woman away with them. They listened to
the echo of footsteps on the concrete stairs.

When they got on to the sixth floor there were more
youths waiting for them—not close enough to be questioned
but at a distance, watching them. At least a dozen, and
there were about twenty on the stairs behind them.

'Er, shouldn't we call—'

'Back-up?' Shields queried. 'Think about it, Alan.' Crawford thought. He knew what Shields meant, knew what had
happened to Ellis in the patrol car yesterday.

'But we can't just do nothing!' he blurted out.

Shields was smiling, not at him, but at their reception
committee. It wasn't a very nice smile.

'There's something to be said about having friends in
high places,' he murmured. 'Have you forgotten, Alan?'
They were moving slowly along the walkway. 'Who lives
at 621?'

'Billie Morgan! But d'you think she'll let you—us—in?'
The opposing group were backing up more slowly now.
The ones in front were younger, patently unarmed, but
Crawford thought he saw at least one baseball bat in the
hands of the rearguard. He knew the theory—he had seen
it often enough in action—the first to be hurt, the innocent
victims, would be little more than children.

Crawford's back itched. He didn't look round, but he
knew that the larger group had come forward from the
stairs. This was stupid, the guv'nor *had* to call for help,
whatever happened afterwards.

Suddenly it was all happening now.

They were within a few yards of Billie's door when the
rush started, Shields issuing a rapid mouthful of succinct
instructions that had Crawford hammering on the door,
leaving Shields to stand his ground.

As a plan it left a lot to be desired.

Aware of the crowd outside, Billie Morgan at first

thought that she was under attack. It was a few moments before she distinguished the words being shouted through her letter-box, and with the words, the voice.

'Get in!' She dragged the door open and the man inside with bewildering speed and was in the process of refastening the safety-chain when Alan Crawford started swearing at her. Even then, time was lost as he struggled with the unfamiliar catch.

'You bitch! You stupid, brainless bitch!' He pushed her out of the way.

When he finally got the door open, the crowd had scattered, satisfied with their handiwork.

CHAPTER 4

Shields lay in a heap against the wall by Billie's door. In his haste to get his colleague to safety, Crawford was dragging him by the arm—Billie cried out as she saw his head scrape against the bricks.

She thought at first he was unconscious, but as Sergeant Crawford lowered him to the floor, Shields moaned softly and brought his knees up. His head was bleeding sluggishly and his coat was torn. Arms cramped about his body, he moaned again in pain.

Crawford was calling headquarters on his personal radio, and interrupted himself to swear at Billie again.

'Do something, can't you?' he snarled at her.

Billie was trained in first aid, but this situation was unlike any she had ever encountered. David Shields was a man she respected and admired, not least for his self-possession and masculine strength. For such a man to be lying helpless at her feet, his head on her kitchen floor—she thought for a dreadful moment that she was going to faint. Violence on the film or TV screen she could take, and even be excited by—but there was nothing romantic about Shields's condition, his tortured breathing or his sweating face.

'Look, calm down, Alan,' Sergeant Pickering was saying. 'Are you in any immediate danger?' He put his hand over the mouthpiece of the phone to instruct someone to alert Chief Superintendent Wetherell.

'They're not exactly breaking the door down,' Crawford admitted grudgingly. 'But they won't have gone far. They beat up on the guv'nor, then scattered.'

'What's Shields's condition, now?'

Crawford glanced round. 'He's being sick,' he said

tersely. 'I told you, we need back-up and we need an ambulance.'

'What's happening, Len?' Chief Superintendent Wetherell walked into the office, looking worried.

'Right. Hold on a minute, Alan.' Pickering gave the Superintendent a quick rundown of developments. 'It's Shields and Crawford, making some inquiries at the Fleetway and got jumped by a gang of youths. Shields has been hurt.' Pickering explained that they had been able to take shelter in the social worker's flat.

'The Fleetway!' Wetherell said nothing more, but his expression was such that Pickering thanked his lucky stars he had had nothing to do with the shambles.

'Sergeant Crawford is asking for help, sir,' he volunteered.

'Crawford is asking for his cards, and Shields as well! What in thunder got into the pair of them to go round there at this point in time?'

Pickering became aware that Alan Crawford was still talking to him. 'Say again? Sorry, I missed that.'

'I said, what in hell's the hold-up?'

Superintendent Wetherell took the phone from Pickering's hand and gave Detective-Sergeant Crawford a string of precise instructions that included putting Detective Chief Inspector Shields on the phone.

'I can't.'

Wetherell's eyes narrowed. 'Are you saying, he's unconscious?'

'No, but . . .'

'Sergeant, unless he's unconscious or dead, I would like to speak to Inspector Shields. Is that quite clear?'

'Sir. Yes, sir.'

Superintendent Wetherell beat an impatient tattoo with his fingers on the desk. 'What are we waiting for—oh, there you are, Shields. Shields?'

'Sir?' It was recognizably Shields's voice.

'What's all this about needing back-up? What have you done?'

The reply was slow in coming. 'I'm not sure exactly.'

'What's that supposed to mean? Do you need help or don't you?'

'No. I don't think there's any danger. I . . .'

'Yes?'

'I'd like an escort for Billie—she's got a friend she can stay with in High Street for a few days.' Shields seemed to hesitate. 'There may not be any reprisals but—I don't want to take any chances.'

'All right, all right. What about you? Crawford says you need an ambulance.'

'No.' There was a long pause. 'But perhaps we ought to get out of here.'

'Right. Now let me talk to young Crawford.'

They had to get them out, of course. Superintendent Wetherell admitted as much while setting about a process of damage control. A phone call to the secretary of the estate community council was the first step. 'Though why Shields didn't do that in the first place, I can't imagine,' grumbled the Superintendent.

He was calming down. Len Pickering recognized the signs and set about organizing a cup of coffee for him. Eventually Sergeant Pickering and Constable Hopkins were directed to meet a deputation from the community council at the entrance to Nelson House. Assistance, in the form of a vanload of riot-trained uniform men was to be parked at a discreet distance with instructions to do nothing unless ordered by Wetherell himself. He didn't like it, but perhaps they would be lucky one more time.

'I don't suppose you could put a name to any of these so-called assailants?' Earl Kingston, a local councillor and an influential resident of the Fleetway estate had come back with Pickering and the others to the Clarence Square station. An impromptu community council meeting was taking place in number one interview room and the question was addressed to Sergeant Crawford.

'No.' He just stopped himself in time from saying they all looked alike to him.

The rescue had been made in perfect safety, the absence of trouble leaving the police looking pretty silly. Chief Inspector Shields had reluctantly taken himself to the local hospital for a check-up and Crawford was trying, without any support, to defend his, and his superior's, actions.

'Just what were you trying to prove?' asked Billie Morgan, thoroughly upset and looking for someone to blame.

'Surely that's confidential?' Noah Franklyn was anxious for his own skin.

'We are confidential people, Mr Franklyn,' replied Earl Kingston. 'But anything that concerns the estate concerns us. Why were these plain-clothes policemen knocking on doors in this menacing manner? Who were they looking for?'

Inspector Powell, who was deputizing for the Superintendent, flashed Sergeant Crawford a warning. Which he hardly needed. If the gossip was that 'A kid's dead, so somebody's got to be fitted up for it,' to have been asking questions about Willis Charles would certainly look like provocation to the others around the table.

'I think we must agree,' the Inspector said, 'that to designate the estate a "no go" area would be a retrograde step. After all—'

'Nobody is suggesting that.' The deep musical voice of Kingston was implacable. 'But why couldn't Mr Shields have referred this matter, this confidential matter, to us in the first place? We are reasonable people.'

There was a silence.

'I really think Chief Inspector Shields should answer that question for himself,' suggested Powell, getting to his feet. 'In fact it might be best to adjourn this meeting until he can make himself available. By then perhaps Chief Superintendent Wetherell will be free—I know he was disappointed not to join you this evening.' And may God forgive me, he thought to himself, because Wetherell won't.

'Don't go, Sergeant,' Powell said pleasantly as the others left the room. 'Mr Wetherell isn't too busy to see *you*.'

Sergeant Crawford swallowed hard. 'Yes, sir,' he said. He had been hoping his part in the venture would be overlooked. But in the event he got off lightly, Wetherell being too fair a man to heap all the blame on to a subordinate. Having questioned and dismissed the Sergeant, Wetherell gave some thought to the situation.

He would have to speak sharply to Shields—which wasn't going to be easy. The Chief Inspector had a way of looking at you as if he had heard it all before—not an encouraging attitude. Wetherell appreciated his undoubted skills but wished heartily they included a capacity for going by the book. Instead, Shields not only had insubordinate ideas but also gave far too much attention to matters on the periphery of an investigation.

After that he would have to call another meeting to redress the balance between the two sections of the community. Earl Kingston, influential though he might be, could only represent his own kind. Equally vociferous was the Mosleyite faction whose leader, Robert Whittington, would no doubt be round to ask why Kingston's group had had an unscheduled meeting.

Shields meanwhile went home and tried to sleep—his turn was coming.

It was unfortunate that Kelly had on this occasion waited up for him, desperate to talk over their deteriorating situation. When David Shields limped in, white-faced and tight-lipped, she realized her mistake—but it was too late to change her mind.

'What's the matter, Kelly? Can't you sleep?'

'I was waiting for you—you know we have to talk,' she urged.

'What about?' He was flippant, but Kelly sensed that he was exercising tight control over himself.

She was going to say, 'Us,' but thought how trite it sounded. She followed David through into the bedroom and watched as he started to undress. 'Do you want a drink, or anything?' She asked.

'Don't start getting motherly, Kelly, it doesn't suit you. Say what you want to say, and let's get some sleep. I've had a hell of a day.'

'Don't!' She tried to control her voice, knowing how he hated tears. 'Don't shut me out, David. If you've been hurt, why shouldn't I want to comfort you?'

'Because I won't be pitied!' He had loosened his belt and was undoing the last of his shirt buttons. 'Now, can I switch the light off or are you waiting to count the bruises?'

The disciplinary interview took place next day, in the Chief Superintendent's office.

'This is a very serious situation, David.'

'There hasn't been any more trouble?' Shields seated himself carefully in the proffered chair. A bruise on his cheekbone and a graze on the side of his head were the only visible signs that he had been injured.

'There have been no more disturbances,' Wetherell acknowledged. 'But we are left with a difficult situation vis-à-vis the community council. We had members here last night, wanting to know why they weren't consulted before you made your inquiries.' Wetherell listed the people concerned. 'Detective-Sergeant Crawford wasn't much help— he didn't seem to be in your confidence either.'

Good for Alan, Shields thought. It seemed Noah Franklyn had been equally discreet, not admitting that he had
in fact been consulted. 'Alan does as he's told,' was all he
said.

'An admirable attitude. I wish I could say the same of
you, David. However—' the Superintendent sat back and
took a deep breath—'the main problem, as I see it, is how
we proceed from this point. We have to repair the damage
that has been done . . .'

Damage, thought Shields in disgust. He had been the
only person damaged, and still ached in places you don't
talk about. Wetherell was droning on about public relations, but Shields was more concerned with the motive for
last night's attack. He had the feeling it had been carefully
orchestrated, the sort of attack meted out as a warning. But
what about?

'. . . need to revisit the estate.'

'We've still to talk to some of Charles's friends—and the
man Shipley of course.'

Superintendent Wetherell stared at him. 'You haven't
been listening, have you? Not listening to a word! I'm afraid
we aren't interested in Willis Charles any more, or his
friends. We have a seriously threatening situation—God, I
thought I'd spelled this out to you yesterday! Nobody rocks
the boat from now on, Chief Inspector, not even you. Is
that understood?'

Shields said nothing. There was an intent expression on
his face, and Wetherell was reminded incongruously of a
hunting cat. He heard the echo of his own noisy words in
the sudden silence.

'I said, is that understood?'

'You're asking me to connive at murder.' The words were
quiet and matter-of-fact.'

'Nonsense!' Wetherell blustered. 'I'll make allowances
for your not feeling well, but only up to a point, David,

only up to a point! There's no question of murder, that boy is a traffic statistic, no more. Our place in this borough is to keep the peace, to provide a climate of opportunity for all, irrespective of . . .'

Shields had heard the speech before, at a great many meetings. It was something the Superintendent was good at, making speeches.

For David Shields it was a negative start to a day that didn't get any better. Flatly forbidden to make any personal approach to his contacts at the estate, he was reduced to making inquiries at second hand. Even Trace Robertson, who might have been useful, had been permitted to leave —presumably a peace offering to his Uncle Earl.

Shields concentrated instead on Matthew Shipley.

He had expected to find nothing significant about the elderly man and was quite surprised when records turned up a previous conviction. It was few years ago and he had served his time—a model prisoner and maximum remission —now he was retired and living quietly on a pension.

But what was Shipley's connection with Willis Charles? Shields quite badly wanted to talk to him but he wasn't answering his phone.

In one sense it wasn't such a bad idea to spend a day peacefully in his office, but Shields didn't appreciate the opportunity. His aches and pains would have been soothed more readily by finding out why he had been attacked.

Detective-Constable Vernon's report on his visit to Iggy Sparrow gave Shields something else to think about. He called Vernon into his office to discuss it.

'What made you think Willis Charles might have worked for Sparrow?' It seemed an ordinary enough question but Vernon could sense the hidden ambush in it.

'Trace Robertson—'

'Ah! Yes, Robertson. He's away laughing, isn't he? What did he specifically say about Charles?'

'That he was into everything, and that—'

'Into everything—and you translated that as thieving?'

'Of course! We've got Trace for looting as well, and as soon as—'

'No! I'm sorry to disappoint you, Jack, but we haven't got Trace for anything. We let him go—to keep his uncle sweet!'

'Shit!'

'As you say.' Shields glanced again at the report. 'This connection with Iggy: what were Robertson's exact words?'

'Like I said. "Willis worked for the man," that's exactly how he put it.'

'"Worked", you're sure it was "worked", not "ran around for" or anything like that?'

Vernon's hesitation gave him away and Shields slammed the report down on his desk. 'All we know about Charles,' he said softly, 'from a rather better source than Trace Robertson as interpreted by Jack Vernon, is that he was friendly with the pensioners' group, in particular a retired lawyer called Matthew Shipley. Now, think carefully, would what Robertson said confirm that?'

Taking his silence for assent, Shields dismissed the Constable with a suggestion he rewrite the report, sticking to actual facts.

All the same there was a lot to think about there. Could Charles's activities be seen as a threat to Kingston's control of the estate? Shields was confident in his own mind that they were dealing with a premeditated killing, and only Earl Kingston had the necessary influence to stage a riot to hide the fact. Shields got to his feet impatiently, shaking his head. That was the trouble with sitting in an office, it gave the imagination too much scope. He stood at the window, surveying the speeding traffic below—he'd stake his reputation on that riot having been spontaneous in origin. If only he could get out and get on with things!

Waiting for the post-mortem report wasn't easy either. Eventually Shields phoned the pathologist's department to ask if they were making any progress—only to be told the report had already been sent to Clarence Square. Further inquiry elicited the information that it had been directed to Inspector Powell.

Evidently Chief Superintendent Wetherell had meant what he said, and was underlining it by taking CID off the case. Willis Charles was a statistic, no more. His death would be incorporated in the costs of the disturbance, the verdict would be misadventure and whoever had planned his death would get off scot free—in the interests of community relations.

Shields's first reaction had been to see Powell and he was already on his feet at the thought. But at the door he paused. It was tantamount to a charge across open country against superior forces in an impregnable position. With Wetherell backing Powell he was outgunned on this and there was no point in starting a war he couldn't win.

So what could he do?

Shields mentally listed his assets. Alan, for a start, would do anything Shields asked and not stop to consider the implications. So probably would Kevin Mann, once he was back on duty. Billie Morgan might help too—but Shields didn't want to ask any favours of Billie. The memory of last night, his helplessness and her embarrassment, made his cheeks burn. He didn't even want to see her again, still less ask anything of her.

Jack Vernon would do what looked likeliest to further his career—Shields considered him not a bad detective but a thoroughly bad policeman. He might be useful in a limited sense. Idly Shields speculated on his potential value as a source of disinformation for the uniform branch.

In a calmer moment he might have realized what he was doing, and been repulsed by the necessary subterfuge. But still feeling unwell, and to some extent a laughing-stock among his colleagues, his judgement wasn't at its most clear. In any case, there was one ally he hadn't allowed for.

'I wasn't sure if you'd be in?' Jennifer Bidwell came quietly into Shields's office and put a file on his desk.

'What's that?' His tone was cold.

'I thought you might be interested . . .'

'In what?'

I've been helping Norman Powell to collate the riot material—we've had reports from a variety of sources, and I thought . . .'

'Get to the point, Jen.'

'If you're not feeling well you'd be better off going home,' she began unwisely.

'My feelings are my own concern,' he said, after a chilling pause. 'I'd still like to know what you've come about.'

Bidwell pushed the file towards him. 'I thought, Chief Inspector, that you'd want to follow the inquiries about Willis Charles's death. I told you, I've been collating the reports—I've made a copy of the post-mortem for you, as well as the forensic report on the car. Of course, if you don't . . .'

Shields grabbed the file in both hands, in case she was thinking of taking it away again. Then reluctantly he smiled, and relaxed. 'Why don't you sit down?' he asked.

'Some of us have got work to do.' The words were spoken lightly, without offence. 'But if you want to talk about—anything, when you've had a good look at those reports?'

'Right. And thanks, Jen. I owe you one.'

'I won't forget.'

The forensic report on the overturned Renault was disappointing. No, the victim's fingerprints were not on the wheel, but neither were anyone else's—plenty of smudges, that was all. And of course the owner's prints, scattered over the rest of the car. More smudges on the outside. To Shields the idea that the rioters had worn gloves was just further evidence of premeditation, but he knew what Superintendent Wetherell would make of it.

More intriguing was the eagerly awaited result of the post-mortem on Willis Charles. Fatal injuries including fractured skull, broken neck—no indication that he hadn't died where he had been found. But the head injuries were extensive and there had been some bleeding in the brain before the victim died.

It was a relief when the day was over.

Mrs Charles paused to look in the shop window.

It was a florist's shop, exuberant with late spring flowers, a riot of colour and perfume. She wondered who had money to buy such things, but the shop was situated handy to the hospital and made a reasonable living for its owner. Mrs Charles was out of her usual way, having decided to visit Clarence Square police station to find out when she could arrange for Willis's funeral.

She stared longingly at the flowers. She had her next month's rent money in her purse and wondered how many of the flowers it might buy. There were roses, long-stemmed buds in a deep extravagant red, but they were expensive. Probably the multicoloured anemones would be better value. That was what she would do, arrange for the funeral and order as many flowers as her money would run to.

The policeman was very sympathetic.

He seemed to be a high-up one, smart in his uniform and silver haired. She had been passed from hand to hand as one after another proved unable to cope with her desperate grief. She had been given a cup of tea.

'It's quite usual in a situation like this, Mrs Charles,' the calm, soothing voice was saying. 'We will of course let you know as soon as a decision has been reached, but I'm afraid we are not in a position to release your son's body at present.' He went on speaking, but the word 'body' seemed so final that she stopped listening. Besides it was getting late.

Hurrying back the way she had come, Mrs Charles came to the florists again. Of course, there was no need to hurry home, was there? Disoriented, she went in, meaning just to smell the perfume of the red roses—but ended up asking the price.

They had been quite nice about it, she thought, trudging slowly back towards her High Street flat. They didn't seem to mind her smelling their roses, the girl behind the counter had even offered to sell her just one rose, and she had been sorely tempted.

But at the back of Mrs Charles's mind was the feeling that she might need the money for something else . . .

The flat smelled of cold bacon fat with a hint of curry in the background. Normally she didn't notice it, but now she contrasted it with the riot of flowers she had left behind. It was cold, it was shabby, most of all it was empty.

She put her purchases on the kitchen table—the bottle of sweet sherry, the packet of headache tablets—worried that they might not be enough. Then she remembered the pills she had taken from Willis when he was acting strangely. They were still there at the back of the drawer, a handful of what looked like pink jelly-beans.

CHAPTER 5

By the end of the week they had made no further progress, but the community was becoming more settled.

It had been Billie Morgan's misfortune to be the finder of Mrs Charles's body and she was inclined to blame the police for this further tragedy—a foreseeable result of their inaction. She said as much to Noah Franklyn as they waited for the start of the promised public meeting, held in the somewhat dilapidated Wallsden town hall.

Rather more well-attended than usual, it looked like being an entertaining evening. Already the meeting had been postponed twice in the interests of continuing peace and quiet. Billie thought that might have had a contrary effect—certainly the Mosleyites were out in force and she noticed Trace Robertson had brought his more senior gang members along with him. They had ranged themselves around the back of the hall, looming large and trying to look threatening.

As usual, Chief Superintendent Wetherell was scheduled to speak, as was Earl Kingston. His opposite number, Robert Whittington, was also to have some time—not because he was likely to bring up anything constructive but because he insisted that the meeting at Clarence Square had been subversive in its one-sidedness. The police needed to be seen to be impartial.

Billie had seen David Shields come in earlier, when the hall was barely half full. She had even made a move in his direction—she felt they had things to discuss—only to find his eyes passing over her face almost without recognition. He had seen her, she knew, but their friendship was over.

Bitterly she watched as he joined the others on the platform. So he too was here to speak.

It fell to Chief Superintendent Wetherell to set the tone of the meeting. An impressive figure in his smart uniform, his silver hair gleaming in the light, he was seated at the centre of the table on its raised platform, between the representatives of the disparate groups. Big with themes of reconciliation and progress, he stood to open the meeting, outlining the perceived causes of the recent disturbance, suggesting how wrongs could be righted. He went on to claim that the speedy settlement of the affray would be balanced by a speedy settlement of grievances. Then he said the same thing all over again in different, and longer, words.

Only after that was it considered safe for Robert Whittington to speak.

An earnest-looking man, sandy-haired and in his late forties, Whittington was a self-styled patriot. In another day and age he would have been a charismatic leader of a disadvantaged people, but modern politics had ensured that his crusade was led against a people even more disadvantaged than his own. Accepting the label 'racist' as a complimentary term, he pleaded the cause of the English minority, swamped by a foreign culture in their own homeland. Less overtly crude than many of his followers, his speech was dispassionate and considered, basically a plea for the rioters to be identified and imprisoned so that the Fleetway estate, and the whole of Wallsden, could be made safe for humanity.

'What we saw last Tuesday was a disgrace to this community,' he finished. 'My friends, mindless violence is not the English way. The English way is to sit down and talk over our grievances, to find a compromise.'

The old hypocrite, thought Billie Morgan, still smarting from her rejection by Shields. No doubt Whittington's idea of compromise would be to send the blacks 'back where they came from', irrespective of the fact that eighty per cent of the young Fleetway residents were Wallsden born.

Shields, who was seated on the platform and due to speak next, caught the eye of Inspector Powell who was standing near the door. They had drawn up a contingency plan with a view to increasing the police presence if it became necessary.

'Ladies and gentlemen—' it was already Shields's turn. 'I'd like to bring you up to date with events before asking Councillor Kingston to address us.' He had deliberately chosen a matter-of-fact tone, and his precisely detailed and rather boring report helped to offset the effect of Whittington's oratory. He spoke briefly, spelling out the decision that the Superintendent had glossed over—the general amnesty in return for a promise of good behaviour. Those assembled were not to know that Shields had been systematically searching the audience for familiar faces. He had not forgotten his attackers.

It was a good speech in that it held the attention of the meeting, and so held the meeting together. The larrikins who had come in search of trouble, of either persuasion, had difficulty making any impact as the more moderate members of the community concentrated on the speaker. Then it was Earl Kingston's turn.

The first few words made his intentions clear and Shields breathed a silent sigh of relief. Councillor Kingston wasn't looking to prolong the public fight, no doubt hoping for a reduction of police interest in the Fleetway. Besides, he had already gained his concessions. It was not that there was anything known against him—he was certainly not in Iggy Sparrow's league—but simply because of his standing in the community the police considered he had to know something of any illegal activities going on. Shields's suspicion was that his nephew's gang doubled as some sort of Tenth Legion.

Shields returned to scanning the audience, with interest. He saw that Ron Purvis had turned up—the white-haired man with him would be Mr Dick, the do-gooder. Shields had met him briefly, an elderly man with an intense interest in other people's concerns. Shields wondered if by any chance Matthew Shipley was among the crowd. They still hadn't managed to get in contact with him.

A movement at the back of the hall caught his attention —the youth who had come across to speak to Trace Robertson looked suddenly familiar. The setting might be different but Shields had a mental picture of him with a baseball bat in his hand.

The meeting livened up a little with questions from the floor. Billie Morgan wanted to know what was being done about the death of Willis Charles. 'Or are the police going to forget about it, now that his mother has killed herself?'

Shields felt that it was a question designed to embarrass him personally, and only momentarily checked that the Superintendent didn't want to waffle round it, before getting to his feet.

'Inquiries into the killing of Willis Charles are continuing,' he said. After waiting for comments, he added into the sudden silence, 'We are still waiting for his friends to come forward with further information.'

He didn't need to see Wetherell's face to sense his disapprobation but was interested to see signs of dismay on faces among the audience.

'It was as funny as a fight.' Constable Wilkes helped himself to another grape. 'There was the DCI, the only cool, calm and collected person in the room. The Super couldn't say anything without implying we'd decided on a cover-up, but if looks could kill, Shields would've dropped down dead.'

Constable Ellis laughed. He appreciated Wilkes coming along to visit him again, even though he was due out of hospital the next day. He asked if there had been much of a row, afterwards.

'Mr Wetherell went straight back, but us odds and sods had to see the meeting cleared up and tidy with no trouble. Mind you, they were a bit stunned, especially Kingston's lot.'

'But I thought they would have welcomed an inquiry, the kid being one of theirs.'

Tim Wilkes shook his head. 'He didn't live on the Fleetway. Anyway, they'd more or less agreed that it was mostly Fleetway gangs that were turning over the cars, and looting—Trace Robertson was involved in that. Well, the Super and Kingston were dickering about an amnesty, like I told you. But if Willis Charles was in the Renault when it went over, then it's Kingston's people that are going to look guilty.'

'So what's the DCI's game?'

Wilkes shook his head. 'Shields doesn't go in for team sports. What I've heard is that he and our Biddy think the kid was murdered, then put in the car after the riot.'

Geoff Ellis looked startled. 'Inspector Bidwell goes along with it?'

'Something she said apparently gave him the idea. Not that she's arguing with the Super, Shields is on his own in that department.'

'He won't win.' Ellis was definite about that. 'Oh, I know he's a good enough bloke in his way—and he could run rings round the Super in the brains department. But Weathercock didn't get his nickname for nothing. The thing is,' he explained confidentially, 'it's the Super who knows what the top bods have in mind . . .'

Tim Wilkes couldn't disagree with that, but thought all the same that Shields would find a way out.

They spent the next few minutes arguing amicably over the likely outcome.

Although Wilkes had logged off duty when at last the community council meeting ended and the various parties had been seen off the premises, Shields had taken the opportunity for an informal talk with Trace Robertson. In his uncle's presence, of course. The rest of the gang had slipped away by then. Shields had offered to drive them both home, but only Councillor Kingston had accepted his offer. Trace's street credit was good but would hardly survive being seen in such company.

'It's no good Shields busting a gut to prove it was murder,' Wilkes summed up, 'because if it's down to the blacks Wetherell won't let him touch it for fear of being called racist. And if it's down to Whittington's mob we'll have another riot on our hands. Either way the tabloids'll have a field day.' He got up to go. 'But there's going to be ructions tomorrow that's for sure. Shields won't take kindly to having it all spelled out.'

That morning being Sunday, there was no danger of the Chief Inspector having an immediate confrontation with the Chief Superintendent.

Shields had come home, as occasionally happened, to an empty flat, but it was only when he was foraging in the kitchen for his breakfast that he noticed just how empty it was. Familiar items that he generally took for granted now intruded by their absence. He stared at the empty cupboard which usually held three or four varieties of muesli and bran.

It was an automatic act to return to the bedroom and look in the big double wardrobe—plenty of space in it now, without Kelly's bright clothes and feminine clutter.

She had left him.

Oh well, he thought, he didn't need her. Shields went back to the kitchen, estimating the contents of the fridge with only one person's needs to be met. It was well stocked, so much so that Kelly must have taken the time to go shopping for him before she left. A familiar sense of irritation crept up on him, he didn't like being beholden. Nor did he appreciate indebtedness, not to a lover.

He had plenty to do, especially now that a few strands of information were coming together. The day only looked blank because he might have been spending it with Kelly. Shields recognized that it was his self-sufficiency as much as anything that had finally driven her away, but there was nothing he could do about that. Being alone meant that he could give some time to thinking things out, especially trying to make sense of what Robertson had told him last night.

But not here. Kelly, he thought, had tried to remove all traces of her occupation of his flat, but she couldn't take away that sense of her presence, the cliché of a lingering perfume. No, he couldn't work here.

'Willis used to run errands for old man Shipley,' was what Trace Robertson had said. 'But he wasn't the only one. Lots of the younger kids know him—there's nothing wrong with that!' Shields had denied the imputation of evil thoughts. It was one of the few social advantages of the estate that most of the superannuitants got on reasonably well with the younger children. It was when these became teenagers that the contact was usually lost—Willis Charles had been an exception, but then, not living on the estate probably made the difference in his case since he was not subject to its pressures.

'What sort of errands, do you know?'

Trace had shaken his head.

Shields wondered if Shipley was a part of that network

of petty crime that made the Fleetway as socially efficient as an anthill. Iggy Sparrow, the fence, almost never stirred from his home, the centre of his empire, but despite the best intentions of the police, stolen goods were never found there. The theory was that the constant turnover of a dozen or so flats gave him the opportunity to store and display his merchandise, but no evidence was forthcoming.

If they could get into Shipley's flat . . . Shields wondered how the Superintendent would feel about his requesting a warrant.

Shields had gone to his office in Clarence Square, counting on the Superintendent's absence—and a small enough staff presence for him to work undisturbed. He spent some time tabulating his thoughts, trying to give random ideas the respectability of clues.

He had one certainty, that Jennifer Bidwell had seen the Renault go over, and it was empty then. He thought about her for a moment before deciding he couldn't afford to get sidetracked.

Clarke, the owner of the car, had no known connection with either Charles or anyone at the Fleetway estate. But there were no fingerprints on the broken padlock on his garage door, just smudges like the marks on the car.

A lot depended on where Willis Charles had been going, that Tuesday afternoon. They would need to see Cal Frazer again. Inspector Shields made a note to send Alan this time, with WPC Mason for company—and chaperone.

Of Charles's other friends, they had managed to get information from two younger boys at second hand. They still had to talk to Leroy Thomas.

But all they knew for certain was that Willis Charles had no obvious enemies and was not involved in anything serious enough to put his life at risk.

Charles knew Shipley, and Shipley had disappeared.

Surely the importance of finding him justified a forced entry into his flat?

There was one vital element to all of this, although Shields didn't need to write it down. Superintendent Wetherell was against turning over stones just to see what was hiding under them. To have the community settled after the disturbance was more important to him than knowing how and why Willis Charles had been killed.

Regretfully, Shields decided that he was unlikely to get a warrant to search Shipley's place. He would just have to find another way.

'The coffee machine's working, for once. Like me to get you one?'

'Oh, hello, Alan. Yes, thanks.' Shields had not expected to be disturbed and wondered what had brought his sergeant into the building.

'I thought you were going home for the weekend?' Shields took the polystyrene cup from Crawford's hand. To call the liquid coffee was an exaggeration, but it was at least hot and very welcome.

'I meant to—but, you know how we were looking at those interlocking circles?'

'You've got something?'

'Something that looked like a merge, and I wanted to make sure.'

'And . . . ?'

'It's Clarke, Horace Clarke that owned the Renault. His circles overlap the Fleetway—he's got a mate of some sort there.'

'Great.' Shields thought for a while. 'Any idea who?' Was it too much to hope it might be Shipley?

'He was seen going into Victor House, that's the nearest we can place him.' They didn't have the resources, or authority for proper surveillance but Shields and Crawford between them had called in every favour owed them in the manor. 'Stayed more than five minutes, that's all we've got.'

'It's enough.' Purvis, Shipley and a few other senior citizens lived in Victor, mostly on the ground floor. Shields thought about it while he finished his coffee. 'Are you doing anything this afternoon, Alan?'

'Sir? No, sir.' Crawford grinned, happy with the prospect of action.

Shields didn't go into details, merely suggesting that they go and find themselves a bite to eat. He was not being paranoid, he told himself, it was merely common sense not to plot against the establishment while within its very walls.

The Ring o'Bells was not much of a pub and tourists, if there were any such creatures in Wallsden, ignored it. The prevailing colour was a sort of dull brown, those features like the carpet and the cushions on the benches which had started life as some brighter shade had faded over the years to become part of the monochrome background. But what it lacked in atmosphere is made up for in service, of a discreet and personal kind. It was in fact more of a club than a pub and Wallsden CID were among its regulars.

Typically, there was brown soup on the lunch-time menu, but it turned out to be quite edible, as were the cheese sandwiches offered with it. The beer was first class.

'We go round and call on Shipley again?' Crawford asked.

'We go round as if we're going to call on Shipley,' Chief Inspector Shields explained. 'If we meet anybody, we call and see Ron Purvis again. But if Shipley's still away—and he certainly wasn't answering his phone up to half an hour ago—then his door won't be bolted, will it? Have you still got that credit card?'

Alan Crawford grinned. 'I've still got them woolly hats as well. We could revert to being the Anglo-Saxon branch of the local brothers.'

Shields shook his head. He had other ways of being inconspicuous. 'Not for me,' he said, 'but it might pay to keep your crowning glory under wraps.'

Shields had intended to wait until the late afternoon before venturing on to the estate, but they were helped by an overcast day that became progressively greyer. Crawford found them a suitable car, not, Shields was thankful to note, a mini but a disreputable Vauxhall of indeterminate age. Alan had borrowed it from the owner of the pub and it was brown.

Outside Shipley's door, in the half light of the empty corridor, Shields again felt a disturbing sense of oppression. It was nothing to do with the nefarious task in hand, though —once he had reached a decision he rarely wasted time on second thoughts.

They had reached their destination with little trouble, not unseen but almost certainly unnoticed. Crawford was wearing tracksuit pants, trainers and a hooded sweat shirt with the hood pulled over his shock of fair hair. Shields was in black jeans and a black fisherknit sweater. Instead of combing his hair neatly as usual, he had brushed it forward, then shaken his head to let it fall how it would— he looked at least ten years younger.

Shipley's flat was identical in layout to its neighbour across the hallway, but there was a world of difference in its furnishing. Shipley couldn't be without money, whatever he had been reduced to in the past. The decent carpet and solid furniture were new enough to indicate more than a pensioner's income.

The Chief Inspector wondered how long the man had been gone. The air was cold but struck him as stuffy, with the taint of long-unwashed clothing.

The tiny kitchen was tidy enough, a cup and saucer left draining—and bone dry—on the sink bench but no food or leftovers around. Like the sitting-room, it showed itself the home of a respectable and possibly houseproud person. Shields quickly checked the cupboards and drawers before leaving Crawford to a more systematic search. What they wanted, he said, was some indication of where Shipley had gone to.

Now for the bedroom.

Shields paused at the closed door, listening to the silence in the close air of the place. Distant neighbouring noises drifted in: the television in an adjacent flat, the muffled sounds of Alan's search.

Then he opened the bedroom door, only to find that Matthew Shipley hadn't gone anywhere.

CHAPTER 6

Shields had seen death before, and in worse situations than this. Matthew Shipley appeared to have died peacefully in his sleep. He lay tidily in his neat double bed, on his back with his eyes closed and the covers drawn up under his chin. There was a glass of clear liquid on the bedside table with an upper denture in it. The curtains were closed as if waiting for a morning that never came. Shields stood for a moment at the foot of the bed, feeling like an intruder. Then he went out, closing the door quietly behind him.

'Don't go in there!'

'Sorry, sir? I was only going to . . .'

Shields took a deep breath, but to no avail. He felt that his tissues were impregnated with the miasma of the death chamber. 'Keep out of it, Alan, there's nothing you can do. There's nothing anyone can do.'

Sergeant Crawford stared anxiously at the Chief Inspector. Shields was unhealthily pale and had obviously had a shock. 'What's happened?' Crawford asked.

Shields shook his head impatiently as he moved over to the telephone. Then he changed his mind. 'No, we'd better not touch anything else.' He thought for a moment. 'You'd better get on to control—get hold of Len Pickering if you can. We need the scene of crime people out here, photographer, fingerprints, the works. Oh, and the pathologist.' Procedures for sudden death were all spelled out in advance, it was just a matter of setting things in motion.

Crawford looked at the bedroom door. 'Shipley's still in there?' He could hear his voice rising. 'He's dead?'

'He's very dead.' Shields had taken out a clean handkerchief and was wiping his fingers on it, as if to dissociate himself from his surroundings. He waited for his sergeant to make contact with Clarence Square, nodding approval as Crawford passed on the pertinent information.

'Look, if you'll stay here—don't go in the bedroom, and don't touch anything else—' Shields walked to the front door and turned. 'I don't suppose you've found much yet? There's hardly been time.'

Crawford shook his head. 'I was looking for something like travel brochures, you know, something to tell us where he is, er, was. All I found was accounts, papers, put away neat and tidy as if they were finished with. Which they were, I suppose.'

'We'll get a chance to examine them later.' Quietly, Shields pulled open the front door. 'There's nobody about,' he told Crawford, 'you can wait out here if you like. I want to see Ron Purvis before things get going.'

'I understand, sir.'

It was only a short walk across the hallway.

'It's the way to go, though, in't it?' Purvis was philosophical in his grief. 'When you get to a good age and go off in your sleep like that. Better'n some of the things that happen round here.' His first action had been to put the kettle on.

Shields was glad of the scalding hot, sweet drink. He doubted that Shipley had really died in his sleep, but it would do no harm for Purvis to think so at this stage.

'Like a drop of something to keep it warm?' Purvis was offering a small flat bottle, but Shields shook his head. 'Oh, well.' Purvis put the bottle away and picked up his cup, 'Here's to you, me old mate, wherever you are.'

'I don't suppose you can remember when you last saw Mr Shipley? Exactly, I mean?'

''Course I can! Last Tuesday morning, he come in for a cuppa—about half past ten, that'd be. He didn't say nothing about going away, neither.'

'No? But you did tell me he sometimes went away on business?'

'He'd always let on, so I'd know not to wait for him, going down the shops and that. He knocked on my door and said there was trouble brewing.'

'How on earth did he know that?' Tuesday was the day of the riot.

'He had his contacts.' Purvis sat silent.

'Go on, Ron. What d'you know about his contacts?'

'I think—hang about a bit, there's somebody at the door.' Purvis got to his feet and shuffled out. Then he shouted back, 'It's somebody for you, Mr Shields.'

'All right,' he said resignedly, 'but I'll be back, Ron, I'll be back.' It was Sergeant Crawford, as he expected, and everything was just about to start.

'I told Len you'd come here to talk to Mr Purvis.' Sergeant Crawford was feeling quite pleased with himself. Without actually lying, he had managed to convey the impression that it was Purvis's concern for his neighbour that had led them to make a forced entry into Shipley's flat.

Sergeant Pickering had come himself, accompanied by Constable Wilkes, to assess the situation. He agreed that a full investigation was probably necessary, if only because Shipley seemed to be a material witness—to what, he couldn't say. 'But if it's a natural death, there's nothing more to be said.'

He had heard Chief Inspector Shields stress to the pathologist the need for a complete check of all the methods that could result in a peaceful-looking death. Pickering grinned—he had also heard Dr Reculver's reply, the main theme of which was sucking eggs.

It hadn't been a pleasant job, disturbing and removing the corpse, and Shields had given permission for all the windows to be opened while they continued a detailed examination of the contents of the flat. By that time the neighbours had become aware that something extraordinary was happening, but they kept their distance. Some, like Ron Purvis, took it in their stride. Their age-group found death commonplace and not particularly frightening. 'We all gotta go sometime, and I reckon slipping off while you're having a kip's the best way out,' was Purvis's philosophy.

Shields had absently agreed with him.

He found himself thinking from time to time about what Ron had said, but it was all too easy. Shipley knew too much to have suddenly and peacefully laid himself to rest. He had to have had some help. Shields's mind was still occupied with the puzzle when the long day ended, and he let himself into his solitary flat.

Once in bed, he lay for a while, letting the facts of the two deaths tick over in his mind. He was aware somehow that there was something he had missed, something that didn't add up.

He remembered that there was a bottle of whisky somewhere in the flat and got up to pour himself a generous dose. He thought about Iggy Sparrow and wondered what connection he might have had with the late Matthew Shipley. Back in bed he emptied the glass slowly and decided that a further visit to Iggy would be in order—once he had coped with Superintendent Wetherell's tantrums. One way and another, he would have some explaining to do.

At 2.45 Shields was as wide awake as ever. He had made the mistake of trying to shift his thoughts into more pleasant channels, returning inevitably to the empty place beside him in the bed. The perfect cure for sleepless nights, and he had let her walk away.

It was no good. Back in the kitchen, in a dressing-gown this time, Shields made himself a large mug of very strong coffee. If he couldn't sleep, he might as well work. He settled himself in the comfortable chair beside the heater and started to make notes.

Had Matthew Shipley died on the same day as Willis Charles? Ron had said that he'd seen Shipley at about half past ten that Tuesday morning. What had the man done for the rest of the day? Or had he felt ill, put himself to bed and never woken up? Shields put the notebook down and stared across the kitchen, seeing nothing but the old man's tidy flat. No, it was too neat, it couldn't have happened like that. But he was aware that it would seem a credible scenario to a hard-pressed Chief Superintendent not looking for complications.

Shields wondered if Shipley's papers would yield any clue to the mystery—sorting through them would have to be his next priority. In the morning . . .

He woke up with a jolt, sweating and hot. The banging which had accompanied his violent and senseless dream continued. Stiffly Shields pulled himself to his feet.

'Sorry, sir.' Alan Crawford waited outside the door, sadistically wide awake. 'I couldn't make you hear.' Obviously the guv'nor had been making a night of it. Once inside the flat, he continued to comment on the latest development while Shields went into the bedroom to get dressed. 'Most of it's gear that went missing last month, not just Fleetway either, all over the manor.'

'And you found it dumped in River Lane?' Shields came back, fastening his tie.

'Well, not me personally,' Alan grinned. 'Hoppy picked it up, they got a call late last night apparently. What's the matter?'

'River Lane,' said Shields. 'Clarke, of course!' That was what had been eluding him. 'You said Clarke had been to visit Victor House?'

'That's right, and we assumed he'd gone to visit Shipley —oh.'

'Right. And now Shipley's dead—since Tuesday? We'll have to see what Reculver says. But if Clarke wasn't visiting Shipley, who was he seeing?'

'Or . . .' Alan's brain was a little more awake than his guv'nor's. Shields stared at him.

'Or Clarke had something to do with Shipley's death?'

'It's a possibility,' said the Sergeant.

Shields checked his watch. 'If we go that way there's just a chance we'll catch him before he sets off for work.' Crawford was still using the brown Vauxhall, much to Shield's disgust. 'Shouldn't you have put this back where it came from?'

'It's a good car.' Alan defended his choice.

'I'll admit you're not likely to get it stolen, but I can't see anything else good about it. And it might have been quicker to go by bus.'

Crawford was silent. He had learned there was no point in being clever with the guv'nor in this mood. What made it worse was that when they eventually got to River Lane, Clarke had already left.

'Pull in here, Alan! Quick!'

It was the first thing that Shields had said to him in nearly ten minutes. They were in the midst of the morning traffic, going north in Oldwall Road. Crawford cut across in front of a rather indignant taxi and parked in a delivery zone.

He wondered who or what Shields had seen.

'Follow me, if you can,' was his only instruction. Crawford watched for a moment as Shields strode back towards the traffic lights. Then he found himself backing furiously in the face of a refrigerated lorry waiting to pull in. He spent the next ten minutes kerb-crawling the back streets in the vicinity. Shields could be anywhere. The housing at the back of Oldwall consisted mainly of Victorian terraces in the rundown state between condemnation and clearance. Some of the gaunt three- and four-storey buildings still housed families but more were squats.

There he was! Crawford caught sight of his boss loitering in the doorway of a rather sleazy bookshop—one that had been raided for porn on occasion. He parked across the street and waited.

'Read any good books lately?' Sergeant Crawford asked as Shields came back to the car.

'You're too young to ask questions like that.' Shields was obviously feeling more cheerful. 'Did you have any bother finding me?'

'Well . . .'

'Never mind, you did a good job.'

'But what are we on to?' Crawford didn't think the diversion had been in aid of dirty books.

'You didn't see him? At the Oldwall lights, that bear-shaped character with the woolly hair? It was Leroy Thomas, the one friend of Willis Charles we've not been able to talk to.' Shields was adjusting the rear-view mirror as they spoke. 'He went into the house two doors along from the porn shop. I wouldn't mind you parking outside the door if you can squeeze in. You know, Alan, the great advantage of a car like this is that it's not likely to cause any panic.' The tone was quite bland, as if daring Crawford to continue his argument—but Alan was too busy thinking about Leroy.

'He got picked up for thieving, didn't he? Picked up at his granny's with five transistor radios—got probation for a first offence.' He started the engine and wondered if there would be time to go round the block.

Inside the house, the man at the window watched the brown Vauxhall pull away. He wasn't particularly

interested in it and turned instead to join in the furious
argument that was raging round the head of the unfortunate
Leroy Thomas.

'You want what?' Chris Whittington was shouting at the
younger boy. 'You and your granny, you nearly blew the
whole scam.'

'I never got paid,' Leroy repeated sulkily. 'Willis
promised I'd get a quid for every one I lifted, *and* get taken
on, permanent.'

'What Willis said don't count no more.' The watcher
took his turn to get a word in.

'That's right,' said Whittington. 'Cliff here's in charge
of recruiting from now on. If you want in, you start by
lifting—and *not* getting caught!'

'And the first thing you going to learn,' said Cliff threat-
eningly, 'is you don't never come round here. Otherwise
you get dealt to. You can see me, at the basketball court
—you get it right, we fix you an old minder.'

'The word's got out, Shipley's fell off his twig.' Whittington spoke above Leroy's head.

'It don't matter. Won't take much to find some other old
fool—we get that holy Noah to line one up for us! That'll
be some laugh.

'The next thing,' Cliff continued his instructions to
Leroy, 'is you forget you ever seen this main man. You see
him on the street with the other white boys, you don't know
him. He's nobody. You dig?'

'Then I'm in?' Leroy was excited by the prospect of being
one of them, forgetting his grievance for the moment. 'You
won't be sorry—I'm good, I'm real good.'

Cliff looked at his leader and received a slight nod in
answer. 'Right on,' he said. 'You're in—just so you behave
yourself. But—' he gripped Leroy by the dreadlocks and
pulled his head back—'if we ever find the filth sniffing
round this place, man, you are *dead*.' He released his grip

to wipe his hand ostentatiously on the back of his jeans. 'Now clear off.'

'I can see you at the centre?' Leroy asked from the doorway, his eyes still shining.

'If your old lady will let you,' Whittington jeered. 'Just make sure you do as Cliff tells you. We don't need another fuck-up.'

Leroy ignored the contemptuous tone. He was in! He'd be somebody, he thought as he ran down the dingy stairs.

'You're a long way from home, Mr Thomas.'

Leroy hadn't noticed the car at the kerb, being too caught up with his prospects to take particular note of his surroundings. The friendly voice materialized at his elbow, 'Why don't you let us give you a lift—I'm sure your granny would be pleased.' Too late, Leroy recognized the cop who had originally nicked him.

'You ain't got no right . . .' he began sulkily as he was ushered into the back of the car.

'You've heard of crime prevention, Leroy?' Sergeant Crawford continued. 'That's our job. Taking you straight home counts as crime prevention, doesn't it?' He got in beside the young man in friendly fashion, leaving Chief Inspector Shields to slide over into the driving seat. 'Of course, seeing we're doing you a favour, it'd be only fair if you do us one.'

Leroy thought frantically about what Cliff had said. He daren't let on anything about where he had been—when Crawford began asking questions about Willis Charles, he felt so relieved that he was almost eager to talk.

'Willis, he's not my fault. He must of got that flash car for some joyride. Stupid cunt.'

'But Willis was a friend of yours—he looked out for you, didn't he?'

This was dangerous ground—Leroy didn't dare specify the way Willis had looked out for him. Instead he began to tell them all the good things about Willis he could remember.

Listening, and occasionally watching in the rear-view mirror, Shields came to a decision. Instead of heading directly towards the Fleetway, once Leroy was in full flow he detoured towards the local sportsground, almost deserted at this time. He parked the car tidily, then turned to offer Crawford a large clean handkerchief with which to dry Leroy's tears.

'How's it going, then?' Jack Vernon was late into the CID office and rather pleased to find that Kevin Mann was the only one there. 'Enjoyed your little holiday, did you?' Detective-Constable Mann had just spent time in hospital with concussion.

'Look, I'm busy. Nobody's done any work since last week, by the look of these.' He waved a handful of papers. 'Where's the guv'nor, anyway?'

'Where indeed? But Len says he found another dead body yesterday—perhaps it's upset him.'

'Another one?'

'Some old bloke on the estate—dead in his bed.'

'Len told me about that. They think it's natural causes. But what happened about that boy, the one under the car? I thought that would have been a priority?'

'It might be, but not ours, thank God. Wetherell took CID off it, said it was down to Traffic. Him and Shields are going to have one hell of a bust-up one of these days. Especially after Saturday's council meeting.'

Mann wasn't interested in office politics, and in any case had not been on duty the night of the public meeting. He was a quiet, almost studious officer, and the only thing he worried about was his pay packet.

Just then the phone rang and Mann took the opportunity to get back to his files while Vernon answered it.

'Thanks, Sarge. We'll see to it.' He looked across at Mann. 'That's really very interesting.'

'What? What are you on about?'

'Message from the DCI. He wants information on a house in Workshop Street—owners, tenants, anything we can get, up to and including a few hours' obbo.'

So much for getting the paperwork up to date.

Back in the duty room, Sergeant Pickering put the phone down and wondered what Shields and Crawford were involved in this time. He had warned Crawford that Chief Superintendent Wetherell wanted to speak to Shields—urgently, but had no confidence in the message getting through. The Sergeant had sounded excited, as if he and Shields were making progress at last.

'What the hell is Shields up to?' Len was addressing himself, but his question was overheard.

'I expect he's still looking into the Willis Charles thing,' Inspector Bidwell said, stopping by his desk.

'Well he's not supposed to. Anyway, he's got an appointment with the Super—' he glanced at this watch—'nearly half an hour ago.'

Leroy Thomas approached Steven House cautiously, watching out for more than his gran. He clutched the pound coins he had been given, unable to believe his luck. He was in, really in this time. Speeding along the covered way, then suddenly stopping to reconsider his position. Play it cool, he said to himself, this is the big time. He let his thoughts dwell on the prospect of a glorious career as a snout for the local filth. He would get rich—he might even become a super-grass and be on telly with his face all mizzled over and his name suppressed.

By instinct he had reverted to his normal behaviour, coming out of the walkway dragging his feet, his head down. His hands, and the precious coins in them, in his pockets.

There was a small group sitting on the low wall where the raised flowerbed used to be. He sat a few yards from them, keeping his thoughts to himself.

Jed was there, talking big as usual. Leroy excitedly thought about the possibilities—Jed thought he was somebody, just because his kid sister went out with Trace Robertson. He was always hinting that he knew things. Leroy had avoided him up to now, preferring Willis's company, but Jed would be happy to take him on. Leroy pictured himself on the fringes of Robertson's gang, taking important information back to Clarence Square, being known as their undercover man in the Fleetway.

His heart flipped as he took in the implications of the thought. 'Being known.' If Tony Clifford or the honky got a sniff of what he was up to he would be dead meat. His face wouldn't be mizzled, it would be mashed! His gran would be joining Mrs Charles in the cemetery.

CHAPTER 7

'Just what do you mean by that? Sir.' The last word was a palpable afterthought and added to Chief Superintendent Wetherell's displeasure.

He had not been looking forward to reprimanding the DCI, but having decided that it would have to be done, he had become progressively more irritated at the man's prolonged absence. It was not unnatural in the circumstances that they had got off on the wrong foot.

'I mean, Chief Inspector, that you are experienced enough to know better! Just as you would tolerate no interference in one of your cases I see no reason why Inspector Powell should tolerate interference in his. The unfortunate Willis Charles—'

'Was murdered in cold blood! And you want it overlooked because he was young and unemployed and black.'

Wetherell felt his face redden. 'That's an infamous suggestion!' he spluttered. 'I'm as concerned about the boy as you are. But I won't have the Fleetway going up in flames over his death!' He realized he was shouting and fought for control of himself. 'It would be different if we had even the smallest shred of evidence . . .'

'Would it?' Shields was on his feet. 'Then what are we arguing about? Look, sir, I'll admit we don't know who, or why—yet. But can't you see, we've made some progress?'

'But it isn't your case!' The Chief Superintendent took a deep breath. 'David, sit down, please. This is getting us nowhere. Try to understand my position.' If the man wouldn't obey orders, perhaps he could be brought to see reason another way.

More talk, thought Shields. More blasted unctuous

talk. He felt he was being treated like a public meeting.

'. . . and so you see I handed this case to Inspector Powell for a very good reason. Community relations in this borough are of paramount importance and it's my responsibility to . . .'

Get to the bottom line, you old fool, thought Shields, savagely. He wondered what it would be like to have total autonomy, to be so senior that nobody could tell him what to do.

'. . . and in the circumstances I'm afraid that decision is final. So if you do have any evidence, I'd like you to turn it over to Inspector Powell, who will . . .'

'You want me to what?' Shields could hardly believe his ears. The idea that Powell could do better was laughable, only he'd never felt less like laughing. 'What d'you suppose Powell can do?' Shields added rudely.

'Inspector Powell can at least be relied upon to obey orders! I want no more upheaval on the estate, David. We have the situation of one accidental and one natural death. Both upsetting enough without your floundering around looking for motives.'

Shields stared at Wetherell for a moment, then, without saying anything further, got up to go.

'I haven't finished, Chief Inspector. Please sit down!' The flow of his own eloquence had, as usual, restored the Superintendent's confidence in himself and his authority. Shields would do as he was told, the inconvenient deaths would cause no more ripples and he could concentrate on what really mattered.

But Shields didn't sit down. Instead he walked out of the office, slamming the door behind him with such force that it was heard all through the building.

Matthew Shipley's papers had been left in his flat, after a cursory examination by the police. The general consensus was that this was a natural death—Shipley's own doctor had provided the information that his patient had a heart condition. There was no point in getting involved in the dead man's financial affairs.

Chief Inspector Shields went alone to Victor House, not bothering to inform his colleagues. Alan Crawford was busy heading their inquiries into the house on Workshop Street —and God knows, that was sensitive enough. Shields was beginning to have qualms about the manipulation of Leroy Thomas. Big and threatening as he looked, Leroy had proved to have a disconcertingly simple mind. His grief for Willis Charles had been real, yet easily forgotten at the prospect of easy money from the police. Not that being an apprentice snout would do him any harm, but his erstwhile partners might see things differently. Normally Shields would have asked Billie Morgan to have a talk with Leroy's granny but that was out of the question now. Perhaps he should consult Ron Purvis instead.

Shields had already taken charge of the key found among Shipley's personal things. Quietly, he let himself into the silent flat. He had judged that a routine task, one that demanded attention to detail, would be the best use of his time.

He was still seething from the scene in Wetherell's office, his overwhelming emotion being one of disgust. Childish was the kindest word anyone could have found for his own behaviour—he called it bloody stupid. He had always had trouble with his temper but had thought himself beyond such infantile displays.

His outburst had changed nothing. Powell was still in charge of any inquiry into Willis Charles's death and Powell was unlikely to see their infinitesimal gains as progress. In any case, how could he turn their evidence over to Powell when it consisted of three parts intuition and the rest hearsay?

Shipley's furniture included a handsome writing desk in what looked like solid walnut. The three deep drawers to the right of the kneehole had been left unlocked and Shields took out the neatly tied packets of accounts. He undid the first one to hand and found it was of computer printouts, including bank statements, dating back over a period of eighteen months.

The time passed quickly enough.

It was hunger as much as failing light that made Shields eventually call a halt to his investigations. Now would be a good time to question Ron again on his friend Shipley's contacts. It would be interesting to see how they tied in with what Shields had discovered.

He was lucky to find the old man in.

'Just off to the pub, wasn't I?' Purvis told him.

'I might as well come with you, then,' Shields suggested, his mind on food. They did a nice pie at Ron's local.

Ron Purvis stared at him, closing the door again behind the Chief Inspector. 'You what? Had a bleeding brain transplant, have you? What's Spadger going to think if he sees me hand in hand with the Old Bill?'

Shields apologized absently.

'Yes, well. I hopes you keeps your wits about you better'n that when you're on the job.' He shuffled through to the kitchen to put the kettle on. 'No notion of time, coppers, messing up a man's tea-time,' he muttered. Then he had a thought.

'There's a Chinese,' he told Shields, 'opened up on Fleetway Road. Does a belting fish'n'chips and all.'

It sounded a good idea and Shields stood up, ready to go with him.

'Nah,' said Ron, disgusted. 'You got Mr Shipley's key, ain't you? We gives them a bell and they brings the nosh up here, ready to eat. Salt, vinegar, the lot.' It was a luxury

that Ron Purvis couldn't afford very often, but he had no
doubt that Mr Shields would pay.

He was right. Shields thought it an excellent idea and
said so. Soon they were making inroads into an appetizing
meal, and discussing the late Mr Shipley's contacts at the
same time.

'I still don't see how he knew there was going to be a
riot,' Shields objected.

'He never mentioned the word, Mr Shields. What he said
was "trouble" and I've been thinking about that. Your
health—' Ron lifted his glass to the DCI. The delivery had
included a six-pack of canned beer, not something Ron
generally approved of, but he was not going to find fault
with a free drink. 'What I reckon is that he knew about
the betting shop short-changing the estate.'

'That's news to me, Ron. What's the story?'

'Well, you know some of the little bleeders run errands
for folks on this floor? Willie used to be a treat at it, some
of my best wins Willie put on for me.'

'And you got short-changed? But surely . . .'

'Not me, I never. But I used to give Willie the odd quid,
like, for running the errand—that's when I got a win. And
it seems now and then the kids'd get together and put a
bit on. For themselves, like.'

'And got robbed.' Shields thought about it. 'But how
would Shipley know that, or that somebody was going to
do something about it?'

'Willie, of course. Into everythink, was Willie. And a
good friend to Mr Shipley and all.'

'You're saying somebody set up the riot to deal with the
betting shop? And that Willis knew and warned Shipley?'
It could only have been Trace Robertson, Shields thought.
He put the suggestion forward.

Ron Purvis shook his head. 'I'm saying nothink, Mr
Shields. You know me better'n that.'

'I'm not interested in that side of it, Ron, only in who killed Willis. Surely Trace wouldn't have had anything to do with that?'

'Nah, not Trace. But he's got some mean buggers in that gang of his. Think nothink of bashing a man around.'

Shields could think of one in particular—he still had the bruises to prove the point. But this was getting them nowhere.

Shields thought again about Shipley's meticulous accounts. They included regular, if small, payments marked C, which could well refer to Willis Charles. It was the source of income that was unclear—large and irregular deposits, always in cash. Shields wondered if he could get the fraud people interested. Shipley's background as a bent lawyer might be relevant—he would have to do some more digging there. Then again, Clarke might be able to tell them something. Now would be a good time.

'Thanks for your hospitality, Ron, and your help.'

'Always glad to oblige, Mr Shields. You know that.' It was the best meal Ron Purvis had had in a long time. 'You look out for yourself, an' all.'

It was already dark when Shields got back to his car, and starting to rain. He checked briefly, and reluctantly, with control, making sure there were no search parties out looking for him. Then he set off for River Lane.

Horace Clarke wasn't particularly pleased to see Chief Inspector Shields standing on his doorstep. The timing was lousy—his suitcases were already packed. It was only the fact that he had enjoyed a large and predominantly liquid meal that had stopped him setting off tonight.

'What is it, now? I thought you'd finished with me?' He heard the slur in his voice and wished, not for the first time, that he'd had the sense to stay sober.

'I'd like to come in, Mr Clarke. I've one or two things to ask you.'

Clarke didn't move. 'What if it isn't convenient?'

'Then perhaps you'd find it more convenient to come down to Clarence Square and answer my questions there?'

'Tomorrow.' He tried to sound pleasant. 'I'll come tomorrow.' By tomorrow he would be safe in Brussels—he'd have to change his plans, catch the cross-Channel ferry instead, anything to get away.

Shields was getting quite intrigued with Horace Clarke's attitude. The man had obviously been drinking. Shields found his suspicions hardening—Clarke definitely had something to hide. 'It needn't take long, Mr Clarke. If you'll let me come in.' With actions less polite than his words, Shields pushed his way into the entrance hall.

Clarke stepped back. He switched the porch light off and waved Shields in the direction of the lounge which was spilling light into the hallway through its open door.

Shields never knew what hit him.

'What a man should do,' said Constable Hopwood to his partner, 'is join the CID. They're parked in an easy chair with binoculars and all the comforts of home, doing obbo. And an all-night bookshop handy—Hey! Did you see that item Jack Vernon was reading?'

'Birdbrain,' murmured Tim Wilkes, without specifying whether he was referring to Vernon or Hoppy himself.

Whenever he was on foot patrol he would think how much more comfortable he could be in a car. The trouble was, you forgot just how boring it could be—present company not excepted.

Hoppy was rambling on about the size of the woman's tits. Like a schoolboy in a sweetie shop, thought Wilkes, no aptitude for real life or adult relationships. 'You'd better slow down a bit, Hoppy. With all this rain we could hit something before we see it.'

'There's nothing out there,' replied Hopwood. All the same, he complied with the request. He glanced at his watch—in another twenty minutes they'd be able to take a break. His preoccupation switched from female attributes to hot dinners. There was an all-night takeaway on Wharf Street that he hadn't tried since it changed hands. 'Though the last meat pie I had there was something awful. What do you think?'

'What is it now?' Watching the wipers had a soporific effect—it was a good thing they'd soon be knocking off. 'What are you rabbiting on about?'

'I was just thinking. What d'you suppose they really put in them meat pies?'

Wilkes shuddered. Perhaps they'd better see if the hot bread shop was still open. He'd had enough of stuffing down congealing greasy meals, cramped in a stuffy patrol car, listening to inanities. It was better on the plod, fresh air at least, even on a night as wet as this.

'Hang about, what's he playing at?'

They had turned the corner into River Lane, cruising slowly past a man who was loading cases in the boot of a car. 'Funny time to be going on holiday,' Constable Wilkes commented. 'Tell you what, just turn round in front of those garages and we'll go past again, slowly this time.'

'What the—' Hopwood swore suddenly.

'Well, he's seen us, hasn't he? Now what the hell had he been up to?' The man hadn't waited for their return, instead jumping into his car and driving off erratically at high speed. 'After him, Hoppy.' Wilkes picked up the handset to alert Control to the situation.

'Shit!' Hopwood jammed on the brakes.

'We'll lose him, you fool.' The man's rearlights were disappearing round the corner ahead.

'It's no good, I've hit something! Didn't you feel it?'

Wilkes admitted as he got out of the car that he'd felt the bump. 'It's a damn cat.' He spoke with a confidence he didn't feel. 'I don't suppose you got that number?'

Hoppy had, and took the time to flash it through while Tim Wilkes prowled round the car.

There was a light shining from one of the nearby houses, illuminating the slanting rain and highlighting what looked like a hump of clothing between the back wheel and the pavement.

'Oh my God!' Hopwood had got a torch but it was wavering all over the place. He looked terrified. 'I never saw him, Tim. I'll swear I never saw him.'

'Hold that torch still, blast you!' Wilkes could see more bundles in the gutter.

Then he saw the mangled suitcase.

'Is he dead?' Hopwood asked in a sick whisper.

'Well, he certainly isn't alive.' The relief made Wilkes facetious. Then he straightened up to shake his partner by the shoulder. 'It isn't a body, you fool! You ran over his suitcase!'

Hopwood swore, at length, surprising even Wilkes who had a wide enough repertoire himself.

He left him to it, sympathizing with the man and feeling the residue of shock himself. God, that bloke had taken off like a bat out of hell, just at the sight of the cruising patrol car. Wilkes ran through the catalogue of likely crimes, coming to the conclusion that burglary was the likeliest in the circumstances.

The street had been undisturbed by the commotion, Wilkes thought. Just then he registered the light that was still on. It was difficult to see through the rain, but it looked as if the front door might be open.

'Hoppy?'

'I'm all right. Let's get out of here . . .'

'I want to have a look at that house.'

'Are you crazy, or what? We're already overdue for a break. Anyway, I reckon we could take this stuff and call into the station.' A hot meal and with any luck a couple of hours time wasted before they needed to go out again.

'Shove it in the back, then. I'll not be a tick.'

Hopwood did as he was told, grumbling. He had time to settle himself back behind the wheel before Wilkes came running up to the car. 'Call in,' he said, breathlessly. 'Get them to send an ambulance, quick, then come and give me a hand.'

This time David Shields made no objection to travelling in an ambulance—for one thing, he was still unconscious when it arrived.

He surfaced briefly to find himself lying on a stretcher, travelling at speed. But the pain in his head was such that nothing else registered. He knew nothing of the subsequent search of Clarke's house, the all points bulletin put out on the car Clarke was driving.

Waking in the very early hours of the morning, he was conscious of a light perfume nearby. Eyes still closed he murmured 'Kelly?'

'So we're waking up, are we? Doctor will be so pleased. How about a nice cup of tea?'

No, not Kelly, but the lilt of the voice was attractive enough for him to open his eyes. Nurse Narayan smiled at him. 'That's a fine fellow, then. I'll go and get the tea.'

Next time Shields woke there was a doctor holding his wrist and speaking tersely over his shoulder. 'Yes, you can have a word with him now if you must. But only for a few minutes.' There seemed to be a uniform hovering in the background.

It turned out to belong to Inspector Powell. He expressed

a brief and impersonal sympathy before asking Shields what had happened.

'I was hoping you'd tell me that.' He spoke quietly, trying not to wake the savage pain that was waiting somewhere behind his left ear. His neck was sore and his eyes hurt him. He closed them.

'You were found unconscious in a house on River Lane,' Powell began. 'The man Clarke attracted attention by making a run for it, otherwise you'd still be there.'

'Clarke?'

'Horace Clarke. The owner of the car that killed Willis Charles. We were wondering how you got there. Do you know who hit you?'

Shields thought about Clarke. There seemed to be a strong connection between Clarke and Shipley, but there was something else, something that had been occupying his mind at the expense of his habitual caution.

'I think Clarke drove the Renault to High Street himself,' he began. But where was he going? Had he intended to visit Willis Charles at his mother's home? Shields thought it might be a good idea to check with Mrs Charles—then he remembered. 'Oh no, she's dead.'

'Never mind. Doctor says you're not to worry about a thing. Your colleague can come back when you're feeling better. You just get a nice sleep.'

Sleep seemed to be all he was fit for, sleep and fitful dreams.

It was the middle of the afternoon before his next visitor arrived, and by that time Shields was sitting up and taking notice.

'Oh, hello, Alan. What's the news?'

Sergeant Crawford looked to be a very worried man, naturally enough, in the circumstances. He wondered how much it was safe to tell the guv'nor. He started on the Workshop Road job—they had made progress there.

For a start, the house belonged to Robert Whittington. 'But he doesn't live in it, sublets it to a bankrupt printing firm. It looks like the present occupiers are squatting.'

'And they are?'

'Hard to know. We checked a youngish man out, late in the afternoon. Male Caucasian, ginger hair. No positive ID —yet.'

'Doesn't Len know who it is?' Sergeant Pickering was their standby for local characters.

'It wasn't a very good photo, but he thinks it might have been one of Whittington's sons.'

Some of the more rabid junior Mosleyites using the premises for their meetings? But that was nonsense— they'd picked up Leroy Thomas from that house. Shields frowned. He should have done something about that boy.

'Are you all right, sir?'

'Just get on with it, Alan. Who else did you see?'

'Spiv Tonkin.'

Shields sat up with a jerk, then winced. 'You're sure?' They knew Tonkin worked for Iggy Sparrow.

'Positive. That's not all, either.'

'Go on.'

'One of Trace Robertson's gang. The same man, in and out two or three times. Jack recognized him when he took over—bloke called Tony Clifford.'

Shields knew the name. 'He's Trace's right hand, isn't he? Deputy gang leader?'

'That's right. We didn't speak to him. Well . . .' Crawford was embarrassed. 'We didn't know what you wanted done.' By the time the identification was made Shields had emphatically left the station.

'You're still keeping a watch?'

Crawford shook his head. 'The Super put everything on hold, because—' He stopped, but went on before Shields could comment. 'I forgot to tell you about Clarke.' It was

not good news, but it was at least bearable. The words
that couldn't be spoken—that would *have* to be spoken—
Crawford was instinctively putting off for as long as
possible.

'What about Clarke?' Shields was frowning impatiently.

Clarke had been picked up in Kent. Speeding, it was
assumed, down the motorway. 'It took the fire brigade
nearly two hours to cut him out. There wasn't anybody
else involved, he'd just driven smack into a bridge support.'

'He was drunk,' murmured Shields. His head ached and
he thought if he closed his eyes for a moment . . .

'Yes.' Crawford wondered if he should ring for the nurse,
or something. He shouldn't have come, but he had wanted
to tell the guv'nor himself, before he heard the official ver-
sion. By putting off telling the bad news he had lost his
chance of getting his side of the story across. Now it was
too late.

CHAPTER 8

In the end it had fallen to Chief Superintendent Wetherell to enlighten Shields on what he had missed.

Wetherell had been in touch with the hospital, checking on Shields's condition, and was planning to allow Shields another night's rest before he broke the bad news. But then he learned from them that the DCI had already had another visitor besides Inspector Powell. A young man with fair hair came during the afternoon, he was told. 'Since he was a police officer we assumed it would be all right, Mr Wetherell. The patient being that little bit better.'

It was nearly six when the pleasant Indian nurse showed the Chief Superintendent into Shields's side ward. Wetherell was angry and he was also embarrassed. He liked interviews to be held in proper formal surroundings. To sit beside the bed, like somebody's uncle, was all wrong for what he had to say. He didn't like the domestic clutter in the form of half-cleared dishes on a tray beside the bed, nor seeing the DCI in the guise of a patient. Shields, stark in white and almost colourless, looked more rather than less intimidating. Awkwardly, Wetherell began by asking him how he was feeling.

'I'm all right, sir.'

'You've not let Sergeant Crawford's news upset you, then? I thought you would have been more shocked by what's happened—though he'd no right to visit you without permission, no right at all.' He paused, frowning at Shields. 'I must say I thought you would have taken it more to heart, David. After all, you've been responsible for the man's training for quite a while. What he's done—what he's alleged to have done,' Wetherell corrected himself, habitually fair at all costs, 'reflects badly on all of us. But I would have thought . . .' He stopped, taking in Shields's blank expression.

'He hasn't told you, has he?' The Superintendent took a deep breath. I needn't have bothered after all, he thought. 'Then what on earth did he come and visit you for?'

Shields gave a shake of his head, wishing he knew what Wetherell was talking about—then wishing he had kept still. He was feeling too fragile for guessing games. Why shouldn't Alan have brought him up to date with their progress? 'Is all this fuss because of the watch on Workshop Street? But I was the one who ordered that, not Alan.'

'You've lost me—we're not talking about Workshop Street. But are you saying Crawford was only following your orders?'

'Of course. Isn't that what this is all about?'

'And did you order him to rape a young woman on the Fleetway estate?' Wetherell flung back at him.

'Rape?' Shields whispered. His pallor turned a dirty grey. 'No! It's not possible.' Alan, of all men. He didn't need to rape anybody. If anything, he had occasionally to fight women off—he was very attractive, not least to the motherly type. Kelly would have been all over him.

'Who made the complaint?' Shields asked, quite unprepared for the answer.

'A girl called Carolyn Frazer. Apparently the alleged incident took place in her home yesterday evening, but she didn't report it until today. So we've only her word, no forensic evidence. But I can see no reason for her to lie.'

'She may have had reason to fit us up! You know she's a friend of Willis Charles? We'd already talked to her.'

'Chief Inspector Shields! I repeat, are you saying that you ordered Crawford to call on this person?'

'Yes.' It was true in a sense. Shields had thought Alan might get more out of the young woman than he himself could. Although he certainly hadn't told him to go alone, nevertheless he felt responsible. 'Yes, he was following my orders.'

'No.' Superintendent Wetherell felt the need to stand up and walk around. 'No. I can't accept that. You're ill, David, you don't know what you're saying.' Indeed, Shields looked thoroughly sickened by the news. Wetherell wished with all his might that he hadn't come. That this conversation could have been left till morning, or better still, delegated to Inspector Powell.

David Shields reiterated that Crawford had only been obeying orders. 'We'd talked to the girl but I thought there was a chance she might have been lying. So much depends on what time Charles was last seen alive.' He looked up unflinchingly at the Superintendent. 'I thought she might talk more easily to Alan.'

'Then it is in a sense your responsibility. I don't know if that will help him with the Police Complaints Authority. Particularly as this was not in fact your case. You know, David, I'm all for loyalty to your subordinates, but I wish you were in a condition to give this some rational thought. You'll only be throwing your career after Crawford's.'

'Then you've already decided he's guilty?' Shields wished he could think, but a painful pulse in his head was echoing the ugly accusation and drowning out his attempts to use his brain. Rape. Rape and Alan Crawford. He couldn't get it to make sense. He felt he ought to ask more of Wetherell but he couldn't wait for the man to go away.

'Nothing of the sort! He'll get a fair hearing, you can be sure of that. We've even . . .' He stopped, aware of an unfortunate turn of phrase. 'I mean, we've asked Inspector Bidwell to assist him in preparing a defence, as well as appointing a solicitor for him.'

'Bidwell had experience of this sort of thing, has she?' Shields knew the answer as well as Wetherell.

'That's uncalled for, David. You know she'll do her best . . .'

'But that's not the point, is it? It takes an expert to get anyone off a rape charge, especially in these circumstances. You'd prefer to believe the woman, wouldn't you? Any decent man would.'

Wetherell didn't know whether Crawford was guilty or not. But he had read Cal Frazer's statement—it looked convincing. And in the present state of community politics he dreaded the reaction to her being called a liar. In fact, this was an ideal opportunity for the police to show their impartiality, their fair dealings with the Fleetway residents. Shields would be well advised to distance himself from his sergeant. What a pity he had never shown himself amenable to advice.

Wetherell was glad to leave. Perhaps Shields would be in a better frame of mind by morning. He hoped so. He hoped that Shields would see sense and drop this dangerous notion that he was dealing with some sort of murder conspiracy. All their troubles had sprung from that misguided idea.

As usual, the nurse came in directly the visitor had left, presumably to satisfy herself that Shields hadn't suffered a relapse. He made himself answer her questions, assured her that he was in no pain, and waited. There would be a change of staff soon.

Since he had not had any family fussing round him, Shields was still wearing a hospital gown, nobody having bothered to bring him a pair of pyjamas and make him look respectable. He had resented the fact when Chief

Superintendent Wetherell first came in, feeling very much at a disadvantage. Now, he felt differently about it. There had been nobody to bother taking his clothes away either —they were safe in the small wardrobe in the corner of the room.

As soon as Nurse Narayan had gone off duty, Shields made his barefoot way cautiously down the corridor to where he knew there was a phone, having seen it on his first expedition to the washroom. He stood, half leaning against the wall, banging it impatiently with his fist as he failed to get an answer.

'Pick it up, damn you,' he mouthed. 'I know you're there.' His persistence had to pay off.

'Hello?' The voice was wary, ready to put the phone down again at the slightest query.

'I need a lift,' stated Shields. 'Be outside the Warren Street entrance in half an hour—and don't bring that damn Vauxhall! You know where I keep my car?'

'Of course, but . . .'

'Then use that.' Shields told him where to find the spare key. 'You may have to hang about a bit, I don't know how long it'll take me to sign myself out. But be there!'

Sergeant Crawford was still objecting when Shields put the phone down.

It took Shields longer to get dressed than he expected. It also took more effort. He was just about respectable, though feeling somewhat thrown together, when the horri-fied nurse discovered what he was up to and disappeared in search of higher authority.

The guv'nor was taking his time.

Sergeant Crawford waited behind the wheel of the sleek black BMW that was Shields's pride and joy. He didn't get to drive it often—it wasn't a suitable car for most of their destinations, hence Alan's frequent need to make use of something less upmarket.

He'd had to wait a while, but didn't doubt that Shields was the equal of any hospital authority, even in his weakened state. Even if it took all night, he would be here.

'What's he up to now, I wonder,' Crawford asked himself as Shields appeared and made his way down the steps at the side entrance. He got out of the car to help the DCI and was sworn at for his pains.

'Don't you start fussing! I've had enough of that in there to last me a lifetime.' It had been an exhausting procedure, whenever Shields thought he had won his case the staff member concerned was replaced by a more senior one. But eventually they had given in—they hadn't any alternative in the face of his determination to discharge himself. But their dire warnings still echoed round his aching head.

'Where are we going, sir?' Crawford hoped the guv'nor wasn't planning anything strenuous, he looked all in.

Shields told Crawford to take him home and not waste any more time. On the short and completely silent drive, Crawford found himself hoping that the Chief Inspector had merely had enough of the hospital and wanted nothing more than to sleep in his own bed.

But it was to be a vain hope.

'Come on up,' Shields ordered rather than invited Crawford as he parked the BMW neatly in the basement car park of the modern block of flats. He led the way to the lift in silence, leaving his sergeant no opportunity to argue.

'Now.' Shields had switched on the light, the kettle and the heater in that order. He seated himself in the easy chair and told Crawford to sit down. 'And talk.'

'It wasn't rape,' began Crawford nervously.

'Oh, for God's sake, Alan. Be your age! What I want to know is how, and why, you got yourself in this damn stupid situation. And me. You came to tell me about it this afternoon, didn't you?'

'Yes . . .'

'Then why the hell—Oh, of course. I suppose you were working your way round to it, when I fell asleep? You'd have done better to stay away, as it happens. Wetherell got word of it and descended on me—like a bloody patronizing social worker.'

'I'm sorry, sir.'

'I'm sure you are. And you're going to be a hell of a lot sorrier if you don't tell me the truth—all of it.' He was frowning at Crawford in a most unnerving manner. 'There's a jar of instant coffee in that cupboard,' he added in a milder tone.

Crawford took time to think while he got things organized. Coffee, sugar, milk and a packet of chocolate biscuits he had found in the cupboard. He suddenly realized that he was hungry. Seated at the kitchen table, he watched as the other man took his drink, wondering how long Shields would stay awake this time and what he was going to do if he passed out. 'I went to see Cal, about this time last night. To ask if she was sure about the time she'd left Willis Charles,' he began.

'Start at the beginning, Alan.'

'Sir?'

'Why didn't you take WPC Mason?' Shields sounded weary.

'I thought it would lead to more trouble—in the office, I mean. There was a lot of shit about you and the Weathercock having an almighty row—I thought we were off the Charles case, officially.'

'We've been off it—officially—since last Thursday,' was Shields's only comment.

'Oh. I hadn't thought of that. I just thought . . .'

'You like Anita Mason, don't you?'

'Well, yes. But . . .'

'And you didn't want to get her into trouble with Inspector Bidwell?'

Alan Crawford was silent. He supposed that was part of the truth.

'Is that all?'

'Nobody knew where you were, sir. Inspector Powell was talking about departmental integrity—you know how he goes on. I didn't think I knew Anita well enough to ask her to come unofficially, just as a favour to me. But I knew if she cleared it with Biddy there would be hell to pay.'

'Right,' said Shields slowly. He had been more correct than he knew in claiming full responsibility, it seemed. 'Well?' His tone was cold.

'Sir?'

'Get on with it, Alan.'

Crawford tried to put words in order in his mind. 'So I went round on my own. She didn't come to the door straight away—I was ready to go away.' And he had been wishing ever since that he had. But eventually Cal Frazer had opened her door. He had told her he wanted to ask a few more questions. She had said that he'd better come in, then.

Shields didn't interrupt, but he took advantage of Alan's occasional silence to ask questions of his own. 'Did she tell you why she hadn't answered the door straight away? Did you ask her?'

'No,' Crawford said, 'I thought nothing of it.' He wondered what was in Shields's mind.

'What happened next?'

'She said I could come in, no, I've told you that bit.' Crawford looked up. 'You know what her flat's like, sir. It was more untidy, that was all, dirty plates on the kitchen table. She said her mother had gone to bingo.'

Sergeant Crawford could have done without the heater, he was sweating now, he realized. Surely the DCI could understand that there was no way he could put what happened into words? That the girl was a slag?

'Then I asked her—' his voice sounded unnaturally loud in the stillness—'where Willis had been going on Tuesday afternoon.' He took a deep breath. 'You see, I wanted to find out whether she knew about the Workshop Street house.'

'And did she?'

He shook his head. 'She swore she'd no idea. To be honest—' Crawford took a deep breath— 'I'd be inclined to believe her on that, and the time she says she saw him.'

'Go on,' said Shields evenly. 'What did you ask her next?'

'How well . . .' Crawford swallowed. 'That is, how well she knew Willis?' He daren't look at Shields any more. 'I asked if she and he, er, if they were . . .' God, it was hot! Crawford felt as if he couldn't breathe. He got to his feet and began to clear the table.

'If you're waiting for me,' said Shields into the sudden silence, 'to fall asleep again, you've got a long wait ahead. I'm all ears. You can't imagine how much I expect to learn from all this.' The overtones of sarcasm became noticeably stronger. 'Go on. You'd just got to the bit where you ask a nubile young woman about her sex life. Alone with her in her kitchen—or was it the bedroom by then?'

'That's not fair!' Crawford replied, goaded.

'No, it isn't, is it? And just how fair do you expect the PCA to be? For God's sake, Alan! Stop behaving like an elderly virgin! I take it the girl came on to you?'

Crawford found himself a chair, further from the heater and turned away from the DCI.

'If you're going to sit that far away, you're going to have to shout,' observed Shields.

In that moment, Crawford hated him.

Oddly enough, the emotion strengthened him—it was a more acceptable feeling than overwhelming shame. It was a good thought that Shields, the cool, superior, sarcastic Shields, was going to be in nearly as much trouble as Crawford himself.

'I asked her how close she was to Willis Charles,' he began, 'that's when she . . .'

That was when she had put her hand on his shoulder and said, 'As close as this,' putting up her sultry face for a kiss.

He hadn't meant to touch her, he swore. But she had taken his hands in hers and gently brought them up to her breasts. She had an ankle-length skirt on, something ethnic with tinsel embroidery, and over it a long sloppy jumper, in a dull green. As she pressed his knuckles against the jumper he could feel by the softness she had no bra on. Somehow his fingers, with a life of their own, were marvelling at the hardened nipples thrust against them.

'As close as this,' she said again, and Crawford had pulled his hands away as if he'd touched fire. She laughed. 'Don't be frightened, mister nice guy.' She caught his hand again, his right hand, and slid it up and down her left thigh. He hadn't realized at first, but the skirt was some sort of wraparound affair and his hand slipped through the curtain into the darkness beyond. Instinctively his fingers spread to enclose her naked buttock.

They stood close, pressed together, Alan Crawford exploring all the unseen velvet skin that had no other encumbrance. Exploring cunning folds of skin and soft moist hair.

They had kissed then.

'So you do like me, after all?' Cal Frazer was whispering into his mouth while her hands did incredible things, admiring what was happening to him. 'You for real, mister nice guy, I can tell.' There was so much of her, Alan heard himself telling Shields, and all of it abundantly available. He could not have said how they got from the kitchen to the bed, only that it had been marvellous.

'Bloody marvellous,' he finished.

Later, in the darkened room that was Shields's spare bedroom, Alan Crawford lay on the narrow bed, unable to sleep. At first he had thought that the DCI would be sympathetic to his predicament—certainly he had seemed to understand that at least it wasn't rape.

The girl hadn't even wanted anything more from him, he explained. She had been affectionate, laughing at his fears and assuring him that she wouldn't tell if he didn't.

Shields had said nothing when Alan finished speaking, only that it was time he was in bed. Then he had offered Alan his spare room, only it wasn't really an offer, more of a command.

That sudden spark of hatred had gone as quickly as it had come. An aberration in the heat of the moment. The guv'nor was going to stand by him after all. Dimly Crawford recognized that Shields had no alternative—he would be incapable of denying his principles in public. They had been so close a team, everyone knowing that Crawford was Shields's man. He closed his eyes, knowing that at the inquiry he would say exactly as much or as little as the guv'nor instructed. It was out of his hands now.

Chief Inspector Shields, burdened now with total responsibility for the incident, had fallen asleep almost before his aching head had touched the pillow.

He didn't need to make plans, even if at that stage he had been capable of planning. The young fool had had the sense to publicly deny everything and that was what Shields was determined he would continue to do. What was rather more interesting was the question of Cal Frazer's motive.

CHAPTER 9

'Wouldn't it be better for him to tell the truth?'

Inspector Bidwell had not really been surprised to see Chief Inspector Shields in her office early the next morning. At first glance there appeared to be nothing wrong with him and his grooming was as immaculate as ever. But she couldn't help the feeling that he had taken extra pains to get that effect.

'The truth?' Shields said, finding himself a chair. 'Suppose, just suppose, the truth is that Crawford did have, shall we say, carnal knowledge of this young woman? Suppose the truth is that she was as enthusiastic as he supposedly was.'

'He'd still be due for a disciplinary hearing, even if she was forced to corroborate his statement.'

'Quite. But where would that leave Cal Frazer?'

Bidwell stared at him, wondering what he meant.

'Think about it, Jen. What's going to happen if Cal accuses Alan in open court? She cries rape and we respond with the usual excuse that she was more than willing. Examination and cross-examination. It doesn't make any difference to Alan, he's for the high jump either way, but Cal is going to look pretty filthy by the time the court has finished with her. As for the repercussions on the estate . . .'

Jennifer Bidwell shuddered. It would be a public relations nightmare.

'What are you suggesting?'

'That we deal first with the only truth we've got so far. Which is that Cal Frazer has put in a complaint. Now, why would she do that, I wonder?'

'Presumably because she was actually raped,' said Bidwell slowly.

'Is that the only reason you can think of?'

'What else is there?' Shields might be tired, she thought, but there was no evidence of it. Whatever shaking up his brain had received seemed to have done it no harm.

'Only that this isn't the first odd thing that's happened. Look, for one thing, why didn't she answer the door straight away? I've been in that flat—she could easily have checked to see who was outside, changed out of her jeans into that sleazy skirt, taking care to leave her knickers off.'

'But . . .'

'Why? Suppose there was someone else there, Jen, telling her what to do. Crawford wouldn't have known—by the time he got her on the bed, all Trace Robertson's gang could have been there cheering them on and he'd never have noticed.'

'But—David! Are you saying that Alan Crawford has made a confession?'

Slightly flushed, Shields sat back and shook his head. 'Oh no, Inspector. This is all supposition, remember?'

'I see,' she said drily. 'What was the other odd thing you mentioned?'

'About a week ago I went with Crawford to the Fleetway and ended up getting knocked about—nothing serious, more in the nature of a warning. I've been thinking about it a lot, and one of the angles is that we'd just been visiting Cal Frazer.' As he went on, Bidwell got the impression that Shields was thinking aloud as much as talking to her.

'She was upset about Willis Charles being killed, I'm sure of that. Those were real tears. Alan thinks she was telling the truth about when and where she saw him—but she knows something. Something that she is to be prevented from telling us, at all costs.'

'Surely if you tell Superintendent Wetherell . . .'

'I can't talk to him, not any more. All he's going to say is that it isn't my case, there isn't any case. And that if I sent Alan to see Cal Frazer I'm as guilty as he is.' He nodded. 'End of quote.'

Jennifer Bidwell uttered an exasperated sigh. Like everyone else, she knew about the loud argument between Shields and his superior officer. She also knew Superintendent Wetherell as a patient and kind, albeit occasionally patronizing, mentor.

'So what would you like me to do?'

'You're a darling,' Shields said flippantly. 'Our first need is for time—if you can stall the PCA for a start. Perhaps talk to Cal. I can't do that without the community council jumping up and down. Otherwise . . .' He hesitated, looking thoughtful.

'If it's illegal, I don't want to know,' she warned him. 'I take it your defence is that nothing happened?'

'Our defence is that nothing could have happened, seeing that Alan would never have been so stupid as to go round there alone.'

'I see. That's very good, David. That would get you off the hook as well. Though I'm sure you never thought of it like that?'

She was rewarded by one of Shields's rare, genuine smiles. 'I thought perhaps Anita Mason might have gone round there with him? No? Never mind, perhaps Alan had taken one of his girlfriends along there, only he's too much of a gentleman to expose her to this sort of litigation.'

Bidwell shook her head sadly, wondering just how serious he was.

When, an hour or so later, WPC Mason requested a private interview, Inspector Bidwell was shocked to find that she seemed to have dreamed up the same crazy idea. The Inspector wasn't in the least amused by the coincidence—though Anita Mason had been adamant that coincidence was all it was. Bidwell questioned her closely, eventually having to be satisfied with her denials.

But there was no denying that it would be a way out, and a better one than shaming Cal Frazer in public. Bidwell had a feeling that even Superintendent Wetherell would have preferred the prevarication, if they could carry it off, to a full-scale fight with the Fleetway estate.

Wetherell, as it happened, had enough on his hands with his chief inspector. For a start, Shields seemed to think there was nothing more to talk about. He had reiterated that Sergeant Crawford was only obeying orders in visiting the estate, stressing his belief that the alleged offence had never taken place. He had even questioned the Superintendent's decision to suspend his sergeant.

'You know as well as I do, it's in his own best interests,' Wetherell answered, finality in his tones. There was a tense silence.

'Why did you discharge yourself from hospital so suddenly?' It was a risky question seeing that Wetherell was trying to conduct the interview on a non-controversial basis. Shields was well-known for his dislike of personal remarks.

After a pause, Shields deigned to answer. 'I'd had enough of being fussed over.' It was true enough, in a sense.

'How did you get home?'

'I really don't see the point of this, sir.'

'The point is, Chief Inspector, that I think you've been collaborating with young Crawford in some way, even though he's under suspension.'

'It never occurred to me that you wouldn't want me to lend him whatever help I could.' Shields was still being polite, perhaps a little too polite in the circumstances. Wetherell couldn't escape the feeling that he was being manipulated—the whole interview was being conditioned by Shields's half truths. 'But I've spoken to Inspector

Bidwell—if I can help in any way you can be sure I'll be doing it by the book.'

'I don't want any pressure brought on that young woman,' Wetherell warned him.

'I understand.'

There was little more to say. Shields retired to his own office where he was able to catch up with whatever else he had missed by his enforced absence.

There was information on the late Horace Clarke, for a start. Shields had been told the circumstances of his rescue by Constables Hopwood and Wilkes, but he had no clear recollection of the events leading up to the attack. Clarke had obviously panicked, hit him and fled. Only to kill himself in his frantic drunken flight down the motorway.

Shields studied the reports.

They had searched Clarke's neat and tidy house, finding only the evidence of his hurried packing and his all too evident drinking. His address book and wallet were with him in the car—ghoulish details embellished their reported condition. Clarke had compounded his stupidity by not fastening his seat-belt and the crash site had been a gory one. He had left no diary.

But there were letters—one from Matthew Shipley, a hurried note referring to some purchases that Clarke was authorized to make for him. There was nothing in the slightest way incriminating about it, but it seemed odd that Clarke had kept it. There were several from a woman in Brussels, written in English and indicating a long-term love-affair. She would have to be interviewed, if possible. A more recent letter, in a neat script, had a Wallsden postmark.

Dear Horace [it began],

I appreciate your concern, but believe me there is nothing at all for you to worry about. What's done is done, and, what's more, had to be done. The world is a cleaner place because of it. As for the use to which your motorcar was put, no one regrets that more than I. But you must appreciate that if the attention of the police is drawn to any anomaly, it is yourself as owner who is most at risk . . .

Shields turned the letter over, looking for a signature— to find only the first name 'Richard'. It was seemingly polite, but also, to Shields's mind, politely menacing.

He put the letters to one side and continued to scan the reports. There was a lot to get through but at least he seemed to be having fewer interruptions than usual.

Sergeant Crawford's notes formed the first part of the Workshop Street file. The hours of observation, the teams taking part, the photographs. Shields thought back to the summary Crawford had given him in the hospital, but it was like trying to remember the details of a dream.

The house belonged to Robert Whittington, he read. Of course, and one of his sons had been seen coming out of it —logical if it was being used for Mosleyite meetings.

But this was the house Leroy Thomas had run to. He had told them, reluctantly, of meeting a man called Cliff, nobody else. He'd explained that he was forbidden to go there again. But Crawford reported seeing one of Trace's gang using the house. There was the Iggy Sparrow connection to consider as well.

Shields studied one of the photographs, taken in the dim light of the rainy afternoon. Something was worrying him as he stared at the vaguely familiar face. Something he'd left undone. He fought hard to let his mind go blank, then concentrated on the face again, seeking to associate something with it.

What he came up with was a baseball bat in the hands of a shadowy figure. Leroy's 'Cliff' must be Tony Clifford,

Trace Robertson's right-hand man. A connection between him and any of the Whittingtons would be dynamite!

There seemed to be another lengthy report still to read. Shields wondered if Crawford had been speculating on what they had learned so far, but it would be unlike him. Alan preferred to deal in facts and leave the speculation to his boss. Curiously, Shields leafed through the neatly typed pages.

It took a moment for him to believe what he was seeing. Then he sat quite still fighting the uncontrollable fury that would somehow have to be controlled.

The signature on the first page summary was that of Norman Powell, neat and offensive as the man himself. The report itself was a meticulous account of the recent raid on the house in Workshop Street. It outlined the paucity of the items found and provided a summary dismissal of the operation as a waste of time.

Shields made himself re-read it, several times.

They had raided the premises at four in the afternoon— Alan, of course, suspended, had known nothing about it. It was thought there had been at least one man in the back room but he, or they, had got away, probably by way of the attic and the next-door roof. There was some evidence of stolen property in a bedroom that looked to have been used as a storeroom. Hopwood's eagle eye had found a signet ring on the floor of the front bedroom. People had lived there, the report concluded, in a casual sort of way —there was a gas-ring and a kettle, but no stove. No pots or dishes but quite a collection of used foil takeaway packs in the dustbin outside.

A casual squat, that was Inspector Powell's conclusion. No doubt the people concerned had been living on the proceeds of petty theft, but they were hardly worth police time—certainly the time and overtime expended in the observation had been a reprehensible waste of resources.

'Count to ten,' Shields's easy-going father had used to advise him when he was in the grip of one of his tempers. Then he had amended it to twenty, and it had become a family joke. 'That's a count of twenty situation.' Even now, Shields caught himself savagely counting under his breath.

After a while, Shields picked up his phone and politely requested an appointment with Chief Superintendent Wetherell. He intimated that Inspector Powell might also be interested in what he had to say.

'Once and for all, Chief Inspector, we are not talking about murder!' As Powell raised his voice Shields sat back with a perverse pride in his own chilly self-restraint.

He had made a brief formal complaint about Inspector Powell's interference in his case. He had pointed out that the house in Workshop Street was possibly connected with Clarke who was possibly implicated in the death of Matthew Shipley.

'There was no evidence of Clarke having ever been there,' had been Powell's initial response. 'If you read my report you'll see that we found nothing significant.'

'Fingerprints?' Shields queried. 'The report I've just read says nothing about the food containers being tested?' He let the silence speak for itself, then turned to the Superintendent.

'We need to trace a man named Richard, surname unknown. The letters he wrote to Clarke indicate that he might have had a hand in Shipley's murder.' That wasn't quite true, but Shields preferred not to mention Willis Charles, whose death was still officially Powell's affair.

That was when Powell had raised his voice.

He was supported, in a calmer manner, by Wetherell himself. 'We're still waiting for Dr Reculver's report, David,' he said. 'But I've no doubt it will show that Mr

Shipley died of natural causes. After all, what was he? A pensioner, a quiet, well-respected man who—'

'Who was up to his eyes in whatever villainy is being run from the estate. Theft by youngsters supervised and organized by an unholy coalition between—' Shields cut himself short. Whatever he suspected the representatives of the rival gangs were up to, there was no way he could move without proof. Proof that had already been destroyed by Powell's clumsy action.

'Unholy coalition?' Powell echoed, his tone suggesting that Shields's return to work had been a bit premature. 'Are you sure you're feeling all right?'

'Clarke, Willis Charles—and Shipley.' Shields counted over the names. 'They're all connected and they're all dead.'

'Clarke and Charles were traffic accidents,' said Powell. Wetherell was nodding in solemn agreement.

'Clarke was panicked into hitting me and fleeing for his life. Because we know he abandoned his car in High Street on the day of the riot—he could have been on his way to see Willis Charles then.' Powell was trying to say something but Shields pressed on, ruthlessly overriding him. 'The fact that the boy was found dead in the car is not, repeat *not*, evidence that he was driving it! We know from Cal Frazer that—' He stopped abruptly.

'Yes,' said Superintendent Wetherell, 'quite. You can hardly quote a witness whom you are currently busy trying to discredit.'

Shields opened his mouth to refute the claim, then shut it in frustration. He became aware that his head had begun to ache.

There was a long silence, broken by Inspector Powell, who had caught the Superintendent's eye. 'It's possible that I acted hastily,' he began stiffly, 'regarding that raid. I had assumed that you were still wasting time on the Charles incident. Nevertheless, since you feel, however erroneously, that your department were pursuing the death of Mr Shipley at the time, I can quite see that you are due an apology.'

'Right.' Shields raised his head from his hands, wearily. So what, if Willis Charles was an 'incident' and Matthew Shipley a natural death? Who cared? All that Shields needed to do was get Alan Crawford off the hook regarding the rape—then he could go home and sleep. For a week. 'Right,' he said again. 'Thanks.'

Superintendent Wetherell looked relieved. 'That's fine then, gentlemen,' he said briskly. But couldn't help pointing out how much more easy it was to settle this sort of problem in a seemly fashion when the proper procedures were observed. Just then his phone rang and the two men got up to go as he answered it.

'Yes? Yes, that's—Just a moment, please.' He covered the mouthpiece and spoke to the others. 'Don't go. I've got Dr Reculver on the line, you may as well hear what he has to say.' He returned to his caller. 'I'm sorry about that, Reculver, if you could just give me some indication of your findings, then . . .'

The pathologist seemed to be speaking at some length. Superintendent Wetherell's expression changed from one of complacent expectation to one of worry. 'You're sure?' Wetherell said at last, and Shields smiled inwardly, easily imagining Reculver's response to those two little words.

'Yes, yes, of course. Thank you very much.' As Wetherell put the phone down Shields found himself a chair.

'Not quite as natural as it looked, then?' he asked quietly.

'Dr Reculver found minute traces of fabric in Shipley's lungs,' Wetherell began, 'and concludes that he was asphyxiated.'

'Smothered,' Shields surmised. 'With his own pillow, perhaps. Did Reculver give an estimate of the time?'

'Yes. Oh, do sit down, Norman,' he said to Inspector

Powell who was still hovering by the door. 'This puts a completely different complexion on things. It seems that Shipley died on the afternoon of Tuesday the seventeenth, the day of the, er, civil disturbance.' Wetherell found the word 'riot' distasteful. 'Probably somewhere between three and five in the afternoon.'

'He was an old man,' Inspector Powell volunteered. 'Any Tom, Dick or Harry could have wandered in, he'd got money, hadn't he? Probably a burglary that went wrong.'

'No.' Shields spoke absently, as if his mind were elsewhere. 'The flat was undisturbed. It looked—it was made to look—as if he had died in bed.' Without meaning to, Shields found himself back at the foot of Shipley's bed, noting the neat formality of the scene, the undisturbed bedclothes, the clean sheet pulled up to the emaciated face. And the smell.

'We did a thorough check, though?' Wetherell asked, 'Fingerprints were there, weren't they? And the SOC crew?' Shields had been reprimanded for that at the time, wasting resources again.

'There was nothing that looked suspicious,' admitted Shields. 'What prints there were belonged mostly to Shipley —and a few of his friends.' Ron Purvis had been among the pensioners visiting Shipley in his flat. But if the murderer's prints were there it would be because they had a right to be there. 'We're not dealing with an impulsive crime. This was a calculated murder.'

Inspector Powell looked sceptical, but said nothing. Chief Superintendent Wetherell looked worried. It had taken a considerable expenditure of community goodwill to get the necessary house-to-house inquiries made after the alleged rape. Councillor Earl Kingston was not going to be pleased at a further invasion of the estate. Then he started listening to what Shields was saying.

'. . . by then we'll have identified the writer of the letter

—it almost certainly came from the person Clarke was seen visiting on the Fleetway. All I need is a list of tenants in Victor House.' Miraculously, Shields was suddenly fit enough for anything. 'As you know, I've held all along that these two deaths are connected in some way—we started looking for Shipley because it seemed he might know something about Willis Charles's death. Now it seems that Shipley died first—but there's still a connection there. I'm sure of it.'

'It's possible that young Charles killed Shipley,' Wetherell added enthusiastically. That would solve all his public relations problems.

'If you think it's possible that Charles could have undressed him afterwards and put him in bed,' Shields said doubtfully. He thought of the skinny teenager and the large-boned, well-nurtured old man.

'He might have been having a nap? If as you say, Charles knew him, he might have been able to let himself into the flat, found him sleeping and . . .'

That was going too fast for Shields. That deathbed had been too meticulously staged. No nineteen-year-old, certainly not the friendly youngster Willis Charles had been established to be, could have achieved that effect. Then turned round and casually walked his girlfriend to the shops.

But at last Shields had a case, officially. 'You can be sure we'll be checking everything out, sir. Quite thoroughly, this time.' He thought of asking if Inspector Powell had any files relevant to the Charles case, but postponed that in the interests of harmony. He could afford to be magnanimous now.

There was a light in the window, the bedroom light, the man realized. He waited a little longer, one shadow among many, cursing himself. He had been wrong to come—more than that, he had been crazy.

But to act, even to act foolishly, at least provided a release from the tension that had been building all day. He was unused to having nothing to do, nothing to do but worry. Now the prospect of talking over what had happened, the prospect even of getting her to change her mind, made him feel less helpless.

The door, as he had expected, was unlocked. But he had been on watch long enough to know that she was alone. He made his way to the bedroom, where the transistor radio was playing, but less loudly than usual.

The bedroom door was wide open, and he didn't need to go in to see what had happened. His immediate reaction was physical. He blundered back into the darkened hall and found the lavatory almost by instinct. Racked by nausea, he knelt and was sick into the bowl. His panicked brain had only one message for him: *Get out, get away from this.*

You were never here.

CHAPTER 10

'So in the circumstances, we thought you'd prefer to know straight away, sir.'

Shields hated cheerful voices in the middle of the night. He grunted something that could be taken for acquiescence and banged the phone down. He lay on his back, staring at the shadows cast on the ceiling by the bedside light. For a superstitious moment he thought that it was their acknowledgement of murder that was causing it to spread like some loathsome disease.

As he dressed, Shields cursed himself for not foreseeing this. They had known Cal Frazer had something to hide, hadn't they? Someone else had known too, someone who was determined she wouldn't talk. He glanced at the clock —he had gone to bed reasonably early, exhausted by a day that had held argument after argument. Now it was only just after midnight and he felt like death.

Shields drove himself to the scene. Nelson House was ablaze with lights and already a small crowd had gathered outside and on the staircase leading to Cal Frazer's floor. Earl Kingston was there, in earnest talk with a formally dressed Wetherell—the Superintendent must have been out on the town. For once Shields appreciated his presence, there was a danger of considerable 'civil disturbance' arising out of this night's work.

One and another spoke to Shields as he made his way to the Frazer flat, but he ignored their comments. His mind registered a middle-aged woman whose face was a peculiar shade of grey, presumably with shock. He recognized her as Cal's mother, her 'old lady' who had returned late with a friend from bingo to find . . .

Shields's breath caught in his throat.

Cal Frazer stared sightlessly up at him from the bed. She was sprawled naked on her back, one foot on her pillow, the other leg bent at the knee. Her head was tilted back, at the end of the bed nearest the door. How she had died wasn't immediately obvious, unless the horrifying mutilation had been made while she was still alive. Shields shied away from the thought.

There was blood, of course, the body might have been bathed in it. The bedding that looked like red silk—Shields became aware of a quote from a faraway source echoing through his mind, 'We have a little sister but she has no breasts.' God! He was going to be sick.

He backed out of the room, swallowing hard, and nodded for the forensic team to re-enter. There was no furniture except the bed, and little room for any. Little enough room for the team to go about their business. Shields found he couldn't think straight and was glad of the established procedure that continued out of training and habit, however appalling the crime. He was even glad to see Chief Superintendent Wetherell approaching.

'You don't need to go in there, sir,' he said quickly.

Wetherell frowned at him, but after one shocked glance he turned away. 'No. Of course. This, it's . . .' He couldn't find any words, for once. Shields thought they would come thick and fast, later.

At intervals during the long night there was time for coherent thought. The crowds were inclined to disperse when they found themselves being questioned—the required house-to-house inquiries were already under way. At some stage Dr Reculver had appeared, like Shields awakened from sleep. The cause of death, it appeared of instantaneous death, was a knife wound. More later.

Shields had wanted Mrs Frazer taken into hospital but the neighbours said no, they would take care of her. Billie

Morgan had come on the scene by then and was proving a helpful influence. Shields had exchanged a few necessary words with her, reluctantly agreeing that to be taken among strangers into the solitary state of a white antiseptic room could only deepen the woman's shock.

But the night was a kaleidoscope of fitful images, bright red or deepest shadow. The tiny bedroom and its burden became the centre of the flat and in Shields's mind the blood was seeping into each room. He missed Sergeant Crawford's cheerful presence but was thankful that the man didn't have to witness the horror on the bed. To see the flesh he had recently made love to butchered would be enough to turn Alan's mind.

Councillor Kingston's eyes were damp as if he had been weeping. Wetherell had made it his job to offer dignified sympathy. The community centre, still warm from the bingo audience, was put into service as a temporary incident room, where statements were taken from those who could be persuaded to talk, and hot drinks were made available. There was an atmosphere akin to a natural disaster, Shields felt, half expecting somebody to start leading the community hymn singing. He shook his head, trying to dispel the phantasmagoria.

Had anyone bothered to tell David Shields that his behaviour at the scene had been exemplary, his dealings with the public sympathetic and polite, he would not have believed them. He felt himself to be stumbling from one muddle to the next, wishing he could scream at everybody to shut up and go away. When at last the corpse had been removed, the flat sealed and guarded, and everything that could be done had been done, he was free to try and catch a few hours' sleep before it all started again.

As was always the way, the latest obscenity demanded all CID's time and all their resources. What was worse, the bizarre nature of Cal Frazer's injuries had already been leaked, attracting media attention in a way that no quiet suffocation could have done. When it was discovered that the murdered girl had been allegedly raped by a police officer their tabloid indignation knew no bounds.

Chief Superintendent Wetherell's own superior, a mythical figure who almost never darkened the doors of Clarence Square, made one of his rare public appearances—presumably as a gesture of solidarity with the staff. Wetherell was in steady demand for comment and in other circumstances might have been gratified by the constant publicity. But this was publicity of the worst kind.

Sergeant Crawford received a phone call from Len Pickering on the Thursday morning, telling him he was no longer on suspension. 'At least, nothing's been said officially but the fact is we're going to need all hands. You could say the complaint's been withdrawn, anyway.'

It was then just after seven a.m., but Crawford hadn't been asleep. 'I heard the news on the radio, Len,' he said quietly, still shocked. 'I can't believe it.'

'It's true enough.'

It was a cold sort of a morning, the misty rain looking as if it had set in for the day. Shops were still closed on High Street and Oldwall Road—if their owners sensed trouble they would stay closed. There were people about, but mostly in groups on street corners. Even Alan Crawford, who was the least paranoid of men, couldn't help noticing that the groups were racially segregated.

'Well, Sarge, this lets you off the hook nicely.' Jack Vernon was the first to join Sergeant Crawford in the CID room. 'You've heard all the grisly details?' Detective-Constable Vernon had also been up half the night.

Crawford swallowed a hasty rejoinder and asked instead if they had come up with any leads yet.

'Old man Reculver thinks she died in the middle of the

evening. Neighbours didn't want to talk but somebody said she'd had a visitor, a honky they said, but that could be a cover-up. She's been friendly—' Vernon raised his eyebrows in a knowing way—'to you and Shields. It might be her friends didn't approve.'

'Er, what time was the visitor?' Alan couldn't help asking.

'Around eight, they said. Personally, I'd say it comes under the heading of disinformation.'

'What does the guv'nor think?'

'You'll have to ask him that, sonny. You've seen Shields when he's scented blood. Still, it's got you in the clear and our friend Powell off his back, so I'd say he'd be a happy man.'

Chief Inspector Shields didn't look particularly happy when he arrived at the station a little later. He had to battle his way through the crowd of reporters who had grown tired of the Chief Superintendent's urbane and uplifting statements. They didn't appreciate Shields's 'No comments', either.

'Is it true that one of your detectives was accused of raping the victim?' A female reporter with a voice shrill enough to stand out above the others. He stopped for a moment and stared at her.

'Is it true that . . . ?' They were angling for him to repeat the ghoulish details of the crime.

'No comment,' he said again, firmly.

'D'you think she was killed by her own people, then?' He was tempted to answer that but knew that once he stopped to talk they would be able to put all sorts of opinions into his mouth. He'd seen it done before. For once he appreciated the advantages of Wetherell's technique— telling the media nothing, in very long words.

'You've not been talking to them, David?' Superintendent Wetherell asked him as soon as he got in the door.

'I'll leave that to you, sir,' he said. 'I've got better things to do.'

Wetherell frowned. 'Keep me in the picture, if you please. And you'll need to liaise with Councillor Kingston—that's vital. In fact—' he paused, and Shields wondered what was coming next—'Mr Kingston suggested that he give us a liaison officer, someone from the estate to accompany our people on their investigations there.'

'We can certainly do with all the help we can get,' Shields admitted. He was also thinking in terms of the Shipley/Charles investigation. He wanted the first name of every adult male in Victor House for a start.

Chief Superintendent Wetherell heaved a sigh of relief. 'Good,' he said. 'She's waiting for you in your office.'

Shields could think of only one woman who could liaise between the police station and the Fleetway, so was not surprised to find Billie Morgan sitting waiting for him. Not surprised but not pleased, either.

'Oh, it's you. Good morning, Ms Morgan.'

'Good morning, Chief Inspector,' she replied stiffly.

'It's not—'

'Look, if—'

They spoke simultaneously, then stopped, the tension easing somewhat.

'You first,' said Shields politely. Then as she hesitated, 'Or would you like me to send for some coffee while you're thinking what to say?'

'I really want to help.' She found it difficult to explain. 'Without getting in your way, that is.' Then: 'It was horrible, what they did to her, horrible!'

'They?' Shields asked quietly. 'Do you know something we don't?'

Billie shook her head. 'Not really,' she said. 'Only it doesn't seem to be a personal sort of crime—more like a punishment. You know, "to encourage the others".'

'Because of something she knew.' It wasn't a question. Over and over during that interminable night Shields had heard the echo of his own voice saying that Cal knew something, 'Something that she is to be prevented from telling us, at all costs.' That cost had been her life.

Over the coffee, Shields questioned Billie further. Did she know of a close connection between Trace Robertson and any of the Whittingtons, for instance?

'Oh no. That's just not possible.'

'What about Tony Clifford, how well do you know him?'

'Mr Shields,' she said, 'I know I offered to help, but I don't expect to be mistaken for supergrass.'

Oddly enough, Shields didn't take offence. Instead he told her what he had been able to find out. 'Tony Clifford is Trace Robertson's right-hand man—you might say his executive officer. So Trace keeps a nice clean public profile, except for the occasional looting, and Tony does the dirty work.' Including the warning attack on Shields himself.

'Cliff.'

'I beg your pardon?'

'Nobody calls him Tony, it's always Cliff.'

'Right. So Cliff organizes the petty thieving that finances Uncle Earl Kingston's do-gooding on the estate, the work schemes and the subsidized sport.'

'You can't know all this, you've no proof—'

'How could I have any proof, when we both know that nobody talks to me? All the same, Billie—' there was no friendliness in his tone at all now—'all the same, I do have a brain and I know how to use it. Which is more than Trace Robertson or his precious uncle do! Have they seriously thought how Clifford gets rid of the goods, and comes up with the money?'

'What do you mean?'

As sometimes happened, Shields was thinking aloud, and intermittently berating himself for being so slow. 'Who's the only fence in full-time work in Wallsden?'

'Iggy Sparrow. But . . .'

'But he's politically right of Robert Whittington, you're going to say. But he's a businessman, isn't he? If he didn't know the thieving was being done by Robertson's gang he wouldn't question the goods?' Someone knew, though. Shields had wanted Spiv Tonkin picked up for questioning, but by all accounts the man had made himself scarce, panicked perhaps by the abortive raid on the Workshop Street house. It was no use raiding Iggy's property, that had been tried too often before. But if they could get Clifford or Whittington scared enough to give evidence, then they would have Sparrow cold.

'There isn't that much theft,' Billie began, but Shields just laughed at her.

'There's enough for it to come to our notice, officially. And you know just how much the Fleetway likes calling for police help. But I agree, it seems trivial when you compare it with murder. Only,' he said slowly, 'it looks very much as if it has led to murder. Certainly in Cal's case and probably the others' as well.'

'You think Cal knew that Cliff was working for Robert Whittington? I can't buy that, David.'

'Not for Robert Whittington, no. But one of his sons—the younger one at a guess, Christopher. He's basically unemployed but he's never short of money.'

Billie Morgan sat silent, overwhelmed by what had been put to her. She bitterly resented what she saw as police disruption of the everyday life of the estate. She had seen David Shields as an enemy, but if he was right about what had led to Cal Frazer's death . . .

'There are . . .' She cleared her throat and went on, a

little louder. 'There might be something I can tell you about Tony Clifford.'

Tony Clifford or Chris Whittington. Shields thought there was a good chance that one or both of them had killed Cal Frazer. There were difficulties, of course, in approaching Tony Clifford. Going on to the Fleetway with a view to making an arrest was hazardous in the extreme.

Chief Superintendent Wetherell didn't like the idea at all. 'We'll need to consult Councillor Kingston,' he said.

'That's tantamount to advertising in the local paper,' Shields said brusquely. He was tired of all the talk and only wanted to do something. 'But we can have a word with Chris Whittington, I take it?'

'You say he was seen outside the victim's flat?'

'The time varies, but we've got at least one witness who puts a fair-haired man on her walkway at quarter past ten.' Chris Whittington had ginger hair, but that was close enough.

'Hm.' Wetherell was frowning. Shields sympathized with him—either way the public relations involvement would be a nightmare.

'Look, sir,' he persuaded, 'inaction is just as bad. If we sit back and do nothing about Cal Frazer's death we're going to have a riot on our hands anyway.'

Outside the station there was already evidence of the truth of that remark. The crowd of reporters had been hemmed in by a bigger crowd of angry Fleetway residents, come to see what the police were doing about the murder on the estate.

In doubt about whether to take Sergeant Crawford or Billie Morgan with him, the DCI had decided on both. One or the other could wait in the car according to the circumstances. Because he had decided to follow his visit to the Whittingtons with one to the Fleetway estate.

A few people on the fringes of the crowd took exception to the car as it sped past, but they were not quick enough for their thrown stones to make an impact. Alan Crawford was an excellent driver.

'You're joking.' The good-looking young man sneered at them. 'I don't have nothing to do with nignogs, do I, Dad?'

At his son's request, Robert Whittington was sitting in on the interview, held in the front room of their sizeable and pleasant house. 'Really, Officer,' he said, 'I can't see any reason for this persecution. Both my sons are law-abiding, you know that. Christopher's only conviction was in the nature of political activity.'

That political activity had involved dropping lighted fireworks through the letter-box of their Pakistani neigh-bours, reflected Shields. The older son, Roger, had done time for GBH, which since it involved stabbing a black youth would no doubt also be viewed as political. Shields didn't think Roger could be involved this time—though he would have been ready enough for the aggro, Shields doubted he would be devious enough for the secret alliance with the Fleetway gang member.

Shields continued with his questions, trying to establish Chris Whittington's whereabouts on the previous evening.

'Went to my karate class, didn't I?'

Shields would have the names and addresses he offered checked, but it would be a hard alibi to break. They had investigated the karate class before, after complaints by the Fleetway committee. It was held at the local gym, itself a Mosleyite stronghold.

Questions on the use of the house in Workshop Street fared no better, Whittington indignantly denying any knowledge of blacks using it. His father got even more excited, threatening to have the law on the intruders and demanding to know why the police hadn't already arrested them—'That's if you've seen them with your own eyes.'

It was dangerous ground.

Shields remembered his original impulse to consult Billie concerning the safety of Leroy Thomas. Now would be a good time. Warning Chris Whittington to hold himself available for possible further questioning, Shields and his sergeant made their way back to the car.

'Leroy?' Billie answered. 'Yes, he's fine—at least he was this morning. He's taken to hanging around with the younger members of Trace's gang. He still misses Willis, of course. They were pretty close.' They were on their way to Victor House by this time and Shields was sitting in the back of the car with the social worker. 'What's he done, anyway?'

Shields in reply managed to infer that they were concerned because of what had happened to Cal Frazer. 'She was pretty close to Willis Charles, too.'

'Did you get anything from Chris Whittington?' Sergeant Crawford asked. He had been unusually quiet up till then.

Shields shook his head. They were up against a brick wall there. Instead he told the others why they were visiting Victor House. 'We've found there are three men named Richard, and one with Richard as his middle name.' He explained that it was a matter of a letter written to Horace Clarke by someone who might have had prior knowledge of Shipley's death. 'If you don't mind coming with me this time, Billie, afterwards we can go across and have a word with Noah Franklyn.'

Sergeant Crawford stayed with the car.

The estate was in turmoil, much as the streets they had passed through had been. Small groups on corners, sullen-looking people staring at the intruders. It was a good thing that they had Billie Morgan with them.

Richard Morse was large and bald and in his late forties. His colour made him an unlikely candidate and the sample

of handwriting he provided confirmed it. Anybody can imi-
tate an illiterate hand, but it's not so easy to forge a com-
petent italic. Morse's hand was the joined print of a manual
worker. His wife had not wanted to wake him—he had
only just come off night shift—but he overheard their voices
at the door.

They had started at the top of the building. Half way
down they called on Richard Robinson, who was at home
because he was out of work. He was twenty-two, he said,
and was it true that the blackie in Nelson had had her tits
cut off? Shields and Morgan got out of the place as quickly
as they could, having ascertained that Robinson could write
little more than his own name.

The third contact, Richard Peverill, was out and so they
went down to the ground floor to call on Ron Purvis's
friend Mr Dick, Albert Richard Dick as he appeared on
the electoral roll.

'Come in, come in,' he welcomed them enthusiastically.
He and Billie Morgan knew each other very well, he
explained to Shields as he attempted to introduce them.
'Miss Morgan and I are old friends. I was just going to
make myself a cup of tea—can I persuade you to join me?'

Yes, he was quite willing to give them a sample of his
handwriting. But what was it all about?

CHAPTER 11

As Alan Crawford crossed the desolate space between Victor House and the recreation block he began to wonder if coming out here had been such a good idea. He'd wanted a few words with Noah in private but acknowledged that he might have done better to stay in the car. No stones this time, but the looks of hatred he encountered made him feel unusually nervous.

Noah Franklyn was, as Crawford expected, in the hall. Trying, with the help of a few hangers-on, to tidy things up after the drama of the previous evening. The police team had already moved out, preferring to transfer their activities to the mobile unit where they felt safe and at home.

'Hello, Noah.'

Franklyn watched as his helpers melted away. 'You again? What've you come for this time?'

Sergeant Crawford made himself relax, hands in pockets. There was an edge to Noah's voice that he didn't particularly like. 'Come on, Noah. Don't be like that. You were very helpful last time we called, remember? You gave us—'

'Don't remind me!' Noah Franklyn spoke bitterly, his voice aching with regret. 'I gave you Cal Frazer, didn't I? More fool me. I gave you Cal, and you fucked her then let her get chopped.'

'You know who did it?' Crawford accused.

'Let's just say I know who came round her place after ten o'clock for an eyeful—then left her for her old lady to find.'

'That's not true!' Sergeant Crawford almost shouted, so great was his fear.

'You've not even had the guts to tell the big boss man, have you?' Noah continued inexorably. 'Well, somebody will, you can be sure of that.'

'No,' said Crawford. Noah was making this up, he had to be. If there had been a witness he would have known. 'It's a bloody lie, a tale to discredit us. You don't even believe it yourself, not really,' he pleaded. 'Do you?'

Noah Franklyn continued to stare at him without speaking. He'd always rather liked Sergeant Crawford, thinking the younger man more sympathetic with the struggles of the Fleetway. He didn't throw his weight about like DC Vernon, and he was always cheerful. Had it been anyone but Cal, he might have felt sorry for his predicament.

'You're like all the rest,' Noah said at last. 'You're all for truth and honesty when it's somebody else's trouble, but when you do it on your own doorstep, you close ranks and swear it never happened.'

'I never raped Cal Frazer—' Crawford began.

'Who said you did?'

It was Crawford's turn to stare. 'Cal made a complaint, got me suspended. Didn't you know?'

'Oh, that.' He gave a short laugh but there was no humour about it. 'That was just Cal's bit of fun. She told me she hadn't had a policeman before, but you weren't bad. For whitey.' Franklyn finished stacking the chairs and moved over to a cupboard, getting out a sweeping brush. Crawford followed him, miserably.

'Who else did she tell?'

'You know sod-all, don't you?' Pityingly: 'Cal was obeying orders—up to a point. She was supposed to lead you on, enough to get you sacked, but she wasn't supposed to enjoy it.'

'Is that why she was killed?'

Noah shook his head. 'She was killed to keep her quiet. I know it wasn't you, because you don't have the guts—

the word is you ran like a scared cat. But she had another visitor, one of your people, earlier. All we know is her death got you off the hook. No rape, no fuss, no nothing. And no Cal,' he added bitterly.

'To keep her quiet?' Crawford thought about that. 'We know there's been something going on, something we were hoping Cal Frazer would tell us about. Like who killed Shipley, for instance, and about the gang crossover.' He wondered about trading information. 'How much d'you know about the gang house in Workshop Street?'

'Chris Whittington's gang, you mean?'

'I mean the house Whittington used to meet Tony Clifford in, the house where they sorted stolen ghetto-blasters.'

Noah stood back in simulated admiration. 'My, that's some story you've been dreaming up. You could write it in a book and get it published.'

'Are you saying you don't know anything about Tony Clifford?'

The other man looked startled at the question, but there was an odd gleam of something in his eyes. He was looking over Crawford's shoulder at the open doorway. 'I only know he's standing there watching us,' he said.

'I really don't know what the world's coming to,' complained Mr Dick. 'That poor young woman.' He shook his head sadly.

Billie Morgan put her cup down on the small table Mr Dick had set beside her chair. She thought Chief Inspector Shields was being remarkably patient with the old man, who had insisted on making them a cup of tea and rather proudly getting out half a fruit cake. 'I made it myself,' he'd said.

They went through the ritual of hospitality, humouring him. It did seem odd, though. Billie was used to bumping into Mr Dick at the occasional meeting, where he showed himself to be shrewd and incisive. Perhaps he was unwell, or, more likely, really was upset by the spate of sudden deaths.

'Did you know her at all?' Shields asked casually.

Mr Dick shook his head. 'I'd seen her, of course. Sometimes she'd come across here with Willie Charles, Mr Purvis's young friend. Oh dear,' he mourned, 'that was another sad loss, wasn't it? And what good does all that violence do, in the long run?' He got up to take Billie's plate. 'Won't you have another piece of cake?' he asked, but Billie Morgan shook her head.

'No, that was very nice, thank you. But you mustn't let all this upset you, Mr Dick. We'll need your help more than ever now, to pull the community together after all this upheaval.'

'I'm not as young as I was, Miss Morgan,' he replied sadly. 'I've done my poor best but sometimes I feel very alone. One sane voice in a mad world, watching the youngest and best snatched away before their time.'

'And Mr Shipley, too,' said Shields smoothly. 'That was equally unexpected, I understand. You must miss him, a close neighbour and a contemporary.'

'Eh?' The old man stared open-mouthed in what looked like genuine bewilderment. Then he got control of himself and uttered another platitude. Not long after that, he began to stack their empty plates, saying it was good of them to call, but he mustn't keep them.

Shields listened to the plaintive voice. This was the longest he had spent in Mr Dick's company and, like Billie, he sensed something not quite right about his lugubrious behaviour. By all accounts this man was a fighter for rights, one who stuck up for what he believed in.

Gently, Shields reminded him of the reason for their visit. 'It's a matter of eliminating unlikely suspects,' he explained. 'It would be a help to us if you could just write a few lines for us, in your usual handwriting.'

'You sound like a schoolmaster,' Dick snapped, but apologized immediately, with a return to his previous manner. 'Of course, Mr Shields, you've got your job to do. I'll always help the police in any way I can.' He smiled at Billie. 'Miss Morgan can tell you that, if you have any doubts.' He looked round vaguely. 'But it was good of you to call. I don't get out so much as I used to, not with all the disturbance there's been—you'll find me here whenever you want me.'

He stood waiting for them to go.

Shields took a pen from his inside pocket and asked Mr Dick if he had any notepaper. He was rewarded by a look of resentment that flitted across the dignified face, vanishing so quickly that it might have been an illusion.

'Paper. Yes, I've got notepaper here somewhere. I don't write so many letters nowadays,' he went on. 'I've no family left, you know.'

He sat down with the lined notepad balanced on his knee, then looked round helplessly for something firm to lean on. Billie picked up a library book from the shelf and handed it to him.

'No, not . . .' He withdrew the hand he had been holding out as soon as he saw what it was that Billie was offering him. It was an instinctive withdrawal and he regretted it, changing his mind instantly, but it was too late. Billie had let go of the book, thinking Dick had it safe, and between them they dropped it. A piece of paper fluttered out as it fell to the floor.

'That's no way to treat council property,' he snapped as Shields picked up the piece of paper.

Billie picked the library book up and handed it to Mr Dick with a smile of apology. But he wasn't looking at her.

Shields had moved over to the window and was studying the note, which looked like a shopping list.

'Somebody's bookmark?' Dick asked, making it obvious that he'd never seen the thing before.

Shields didn't answer. It was only a shopping list after all, bread and self-raising flour, currants, etcetera. Shields ran through the items, noting the reminder at the bottom, library. He studied the familiar script.

'Now! What is it you want me to write?'

Getting no answer, Mr Dick frowned and began laboriously to put pen to paper with a trembling hand. The result was nothing like the sample that Shields was holding, but then he hadn't expected it would be. They would probably need to enlist the help of an expert graphologist—unless Dick ended the farce by confessing. But Shields already held in his hand the sample of handwriting that appeared to conform in every way to the letter found among Clarke's belongings.

He cautioned the old man, reciting the time-honoured formula. 'Albert Richard Dick, I'm arresting you in connection with the murder of Matthew Shipley on Tuesday the seventeenth . . .' Shields thought he knew how and he also thought he knew why. There could be some doubt, but he had no doubts at all about who. Friend Dick's fingerprints had been found in the flat and Shipley would have been supremely unafraid of him. '. . . but whatever you do say may be used in evidence.'

Mr Dick looked from Shields to Billie Morgan in obvious bewilderment. 'What is he talking about?' he pleaded. 'What's he saying? Murder? I've never hurt a fly, you know that, don't you? Miss Morgan?'

'This is nothing to do with me, Mr Dick.' Billie was remembering everything she had ever disliked about Chief Inspector Shields. How dared he use her as camouflage like this, counting on her presence to lull the old man into a false sense of security? She didn't know what evidence Shields had against Mr Dick, but she wasn't going to be a party to this. She told him so, in no uncertain terms.

'Have you finished?' Shields asked coldly. The sooner she was gone the better, so far as he was concerned. Then he remembered. 'Billie,' he called urgently as she reached the door. With a glance to make sure Mr Dick was still sitting helplessly in his comfortable chair, Shields crossed the room and spoke quietly to her.

'No, I won't help you . . .'

'I'm not the one who needs help, you silly woman,' Shields retorted, even more angry because of having to keep his voice down. 'It's the kid's safety I'm concerned with.'

Billie bit her lip. 'What do you want me to do?'

'Just drop in on Mrs Thomas and stay there as long as you can.' He glanced back at the window. 'There's a crowd gathering round the community hall—it looks as though there might be trouble.'

'How could that hurt Leroy?'

'I don't know. Let's just say that if anyone does want to hurt him, this would be an ideal opportunity.' The name of Willis Charles lay unspoken between them. Then: 'Sit down, Mr Dick. You're not going anywhere, not just yet.'

As soon as Billie Morgan had gone, Shields made his call to control. He told them he had made an arrest in the Shipley case, and needed uniformed assistance in bringing his prisoner in.

It was a good thing Sergeant Pickering couldn't see the prisoner concerned, Shields thought. Mr Dick was sitting hunched up in his chair beside the heater, his head down, the very picture of hopelessness.

'It won't be long now, Mr Dick,' Shields said quietly. 'I expect you'll want to contact your solicitor.' Not that he would need one—he had no doubt that Dick could run rings round them once he got started. He thought of the man's reputation in the borough, 'Dick the do-gooder,' Ron Purvis had called him and Shields's own inquiries had proved that correct. He was a tireless campaigner for civil rights and social equality, one moreover who had escaped a limiting identification with either of the warring political factions.

'This is all a sad mistake, Mr Shields.' The old man's face had assumed a saintly expression. 'I am not a violent man, you know.'

Shields listened warily, hoping Dick was not going to introduce the subject of Matthew Shipley, who would have been a much more acceptable candidate for gaol. He wondered what had been the last straw so far as Dick was concerned—after all, he had lived with Shipley as his neighbour for several years. Had he only recently found out that Shipley was living on the proceeds of embezzlement? How long had he known, as Shields knew now, that Shipley had defrauded the old and the helpless, stealing from trust funds in his care? Trust funds that so often were pensioners' life savings. Had Dick got tired of seeing how well Shipley lived on the proceeds of his crimes, made one visit too many to the luxuriously appointed flat?

'What's going to happen to me now?' Dick asked in a querulous tone. Shields felt like reminding him that there was not, as yet, any jury present to be influenced by his white hair and helplessness. Dick cocked his head. 'What's all the noise out there?'

Shields had stationed himself near the window where he could glance out occasionally without taking his attention from the suspect. The crowd around the hall was bigger now, composed almost entirely of young blacks.

Shields made some soothing answer and continued to wait. He didn't underestimate the difficulties that lay ahead —taking Mr Dick into custody while the gangs were still at large sharpening their weapons was likely to attract any amount of adverse publicity. Shields had given strict instructions for Councillor Kingston to be advised of their errand, just in case.

The patrol car must have pulled in on the other side of the building. The first Shields knew of their presence was the sound of heavy footsteps in the corridor outside.

The four large policemen filled the small room. Shields explained to the two uniformed constables, Hopwood and Tim Wilkes, what he wanted doing. 'Mr Dick is under arrest for the murder of Matthew Shipley,' he stated. 'But in view of his age and frailty I want you to take special care of him. Treat him with respect.'

'Yes, sir.'

'You've got your handcuffs, Tim?'

Constable Wilkes looked startled, but produced the item in question. Resignedly, Mr Dick held out his wrists in front of him, pushing back his cardigan sleeves.

'Just one will do. You know the drill, Constable.' Like one in a dream, Tim Wilkes fastened one of the shiny steel bracelets about the bony and trembling wrist of the pensioner before securing the other to his own.

Jack Vernon and Detective-Constable Mann stayed by the door, watching the disquieting scene. There was something so incongruous about Wilkes's familiar bulk against the insubstantial form of the dignified old man. But Vernon noted with surprise that the prisoner would have been almost as tall as Wilkes, if he had pulled himself up to his full height. But he was bent over, as if he had some great weight of sorrow to carry.

'What about my home?' Dick asked pathetically as they neared the door. He had stopped shuffling forward and turned to face Shields, still standing guard by the window. 'Suppose somebody breaks in?' he asked, as if that were the worst that could happen to him.

Shields said nothing. Constable Wilkes explained that

the property would be locked up, decided that was an unfortunate way of putting it and corrected himself to, 'Quite
safe, sir. You can be sure of that.'

Vernon waited until prisoner and escort had removed
themselves before telling Shields why Len Pickering had
sent them. 'There's been a swag of reports through, sir,' he
said.

Shields was staring at the milling crowd outside. 'D'you
know if he's heard anything from Alan Crawford?' he asked.

'No, sir. What happens now?'

'Now we go and find out what's happening.'

Sergeant Crawford had known a moment of panic as he
recognized the threatening form of Trace Robertson's lieu-
tenant. Then he looked back at Noah, who was grinning.

'It's a trap! You rotten bugger, it's a bloody trap!'

Tony Clifford approached them alone, leaving his two
or three minders propping up the doorway.

'You hassling brother Noah here, mister longnose?'

'This is a private conversation, Clifford. Nobody's being
hassled.'

'You got that wrong, my man. If brother Noah don't
object, I might just demonstrate you what hassling is all
about. But first, we'nt been properly introduced. Bro?'

Noah Franklyn nodded. 'Mister Cliff Clifford meet Mister Sergeant Crawford of the Clarence Square detectives.'

'Yeah. I seen him before. I seen him hiding away behind
some black skirt when me and my brothers had the pleasure
of chastizing mister boss man. Seems he likes black skirt.'

Crawford felt a chill as he remembered the beating the
DCI had taken at this man's hands. He assumed he was
in for the same treatment, though there were as yet no
baseball bats in evidence. He wondered about his chances
of calling for help.

Clifford seemed to be staring at the Sergeant's fair hair.

'I'm remembering,' he said slowly, 'they was a lot of questions being asked last night, about some yellow-haired man that was visiting my poor Cal Frazer.'

'I . . .' began Crawford, then stopped.

'You? What about you? You going to tell us you wasn't the mister nice guy that left Cal there in all her blood?'

I didn't kill her! Crawford's mind was screaming. I didn't rape her and I didn't kill her. But there was no point in saying it to these accusers. They were concerned with different crimes.

Noah Franklyn was saying something.

'He what?' Clifford demanded.

'He was asking questions about some house in Workshop Street,' Noah said again. 'Some house that got raided.'

Clifford's mirthless grin showed all his teeth. 'You a good bro, brother Noah.' He was staring at Crawford as he spoke. 'I had my doubts, you know? I thought you might have been a little singing bird, hidden away here in your hall and being so friendly with mister nice guy here.'

'It's my job to be friendly, you know that.'

'I know. But sometimes you got to give a little bit of proof that you not being friendly to the wrong man. You telling me what this same sergeant-man had to say to you is my kind of proof.'

'He thinks you been meeting with Chris Whittington, like you've been selling out on Trace and the others.' There was the slightest edge in Franklyn's voice, Crawford heard it and so, he was sure, had Clifford.

What was Franklyn's game? Did he think he could threaten Clifford and survive? Or did he have blackmail in mind? Either way he was making the situation marginally more dangerous for both of them.

'He's a bad man, brother Noah,' said Clifford at last. 'We going to deal to him, that for sure.' He suddenly had a knife in his hand.

Crawford tried to call for help but the radio was knocked violently from his hand. He stared around in desperation. There were about a dozen of the gang in the hall now, though still keeping their distance. But Crawford could tell by the noise that there were more of them outside.

'Don't be a fool, Clifford,' he said, his voice raised in fear. 'My guv'nor's here on the estate. We'd pick you up in no time if you do anything stupid.' He thought again about Noah Franklyn's incalculable loyalties—surely he wouldn't want to see the Fleetway suffer the sort of repression attacking a police officer would bring? Then he remembered the attack on Inspector Shields.

Clifford had led the attack on the DCI and there had been no reprisals at all, thanks to the Weathercock's hands-off policy. No wonder the man was smiling. With the knife at his throat, Sergeant Crawford cursed his superintendent with all his being.

CHAPTER 12

'That's just enough of that!'

Alan Crawford heard the words from somewhere far away. The dangerous game had been going on for quite a while and he was feeling disoriented.

'I said, that's enough!'

With a little thought he identified the voice as that of Earl Kingston. They were outside the hall now, in the midst of a crowd whose size was hard to judge in the fading light. But the bodies were parting, a gap was being made so that Councillor Kingston could approach.

He was not alone.

Earl Kingston had come from being consulted by Chief Inspector Shields, first about the arrest that was being made and ultimately about the danger to the Detective-Sergeant. Only the three plain-clothes men were with him but he had been warned about the patrol cars on their way to the scene.

'It's only a bit of fun, Mr Kingston.' Noah Franklyn pushed through to the front of the crowd. 'Harmless fun.' Sergeant Crawford wondered, not for the first time, whose side Noah was on. Then it was his turn to be pushed forward.

'Mr Crawford!' Councillor Kingston was shocked at the sight of the scarecrow figure. 'Are you hurt, man?'

Crawford shook his head, and felt the blood trickling across his bare scalp as he did so. His tormentors seemed to have let go of him at last and he took a few stumbling steps towards his colleagues.

Jack Vernon grabbed his arm, swearing as he did so. 'They've done it now—we'll crucify the lot of them. Sarge? Are you all right?'

Sergeant Crawford didn't answer.

'No, you're in shock. We'll get you back to the station once we've sorted this lot. Once the DCI's finished playing Weathercock's game.'

Chief Inspector Shields was talking quietly to Earl Kingston, who was preparing to address the crowd.

'These policemen . . .' Kingston began, looking at Shields, who nodded encouragingly. 'These policemen want to talk to Tony Clifford. He's here, isn't he?'

There was a threatening growl from the crowd.

'Of course he's here,' Alan Crawford muttered. 'Who else is so handy with a knife?' He was cold, shaken and sick.

'Take Crawford to the car.' Shields gave the order to Kevin Mann, glancing at him briefly before turning his attention back to Councillor Kingston.

'Mr Shields says that this is a very important matter. They want Clifford to help them with their inquiries.'

'Them filth taking no brother of mine away from here,' Trace Robertson, a latecomer to the scene, was making his presence felt. 'Since when did Fleetway do the police work for them?'

'Since brother Clifford joined Babylon,' came a voice from the crowd.

Shields was still saying nothing, respecting Earl Kingston's control over the volatile situation. He thought the voice had been Noah Franklyn's but he couldn't be sure. Trace Robertson wasn't sure either. 'What that supposed to mean? Who talking that shit?'

Nobody answered. Some on the fringes of the crowd were slipping away, but Shields was reasonably confident that Clifford was still in there, somewhere. He badly wanted to get hold of him, not least for the way he had treated Alan Crawford. His mind was going over possible charges, assault with a deadly weapon being the likeliest. But the fact that Clifford had used the deadly weapon merely to cut off all the Detective-Sergeant's fair hair would make it hard for them to get a conviction.

Earl Kingston was still earnestly pleading for Tony Clifford to come forward. 'There are questions to be answered,' he said. 'Questions about the killing of our poor Cal Frazer.'

'Then the police better answer them!' Trace shouted, above a growl of voices. 'We all know who the last to see her, scuttling away in the darkness and leaving her there for her ma to find.'

'Who?' Kingston asked, furious.

'Who but mister nice guy there?' Tony Clifford answered, out of the darkness.

'So I have no alternative, sir, but to throw myself on your mercy.'

This was most embarrassing. Chief Superintendent Wetherell glanced at Mr Dick's solicitor, hoping the man would advise his client to stay silent. It was not Wetherell's place to interview suspects, particularly not when the case belonged properly to DCI Shields.

Of course, Mr Dick shouldn't have been arrested in the first place. He was a tireless worker for the community, Wetherell knew that. He was elderly and respectable. He was also hell-bent on confessing his crime to Wetherell himself, it seemed. Although his solicitor had been contacted straight away, Mr Dick had pleaded for a word with the Superintendent.

That had been nearly an hour ago.

At first Wetherell had tried to put the man off, he had enough to worry about with the situation forming at the Fleetway. He didn't trust Shields to act without exacerbating the problem. But the presence of Mr Dick was awkward enough without the added snub of refusing

to see him. So here he was in number two interview room
and in some embarrassment. Mr Dick was the picture of
benevolent old age with his white hair, his mottled hands
clasped about his heavy walking stick.

'I beg you.'

'Mr Dick, please.'

'If you could only understand the burden this has been?
Oh, I know your inspector was only doing his job, as he
sees it, but—these young men, Mr Wetherell! They don't
understand the greater picture, as we do.' He waited, took
Wetherell's brief nod as encouragement and continued, 'Of
course, I'd known about Shipley's ill-doing for some time.
But, I reasoned, he had paid his debt to society, he was
entitled to pass his remaining years in peace.'

'Mr Dick, I really think—'

The elderly suspect held up his hand. 'I know what you
are going to say, sir. That I should have made known my
discoveries to the proper authorities. I know that. How I
regret my decision.' In a dramatic pause he searched for
his handkerchief.

Unable to walk rudely out, Wetherell resigned himself
to letting the old man talk. Perhaps he would feel better
for getting it off his chest.

'Your decision?'

'I did what I thought was fair, sir. I faced Matthew
Shipley and taxed him with his corruption of our young
people. I had learned of his clandestine contacts with that
scourge of the community named Sparrow, that he was
leading the young in the way of crime—crime that would
ultimately benefit that bloodsucking monster.'

It must have taken some courage to do that, thought
Wetherell. He tried to picture the scene, but not having
known Shipley, it was difficult.

'So I faced him. I dropped in on him in the middle of
the afternoon. You must understand we were not friends,

but we have—we had—a mutual friend and so my visit was no great surprise to him.' There was a long pause, while the distressed man fought for words.

'He was in his bedroom, but he called for me to come in. He was sitting on his bed—and it was clear to me, Superintendent, that there had been two heads on that pillow. You understand what I am saying?'

Wetherell didn't. He waited for Mr Dick to explain.

'Not content with leading that young innocent in the way of crime, it seemed to me that he was introducing him to degradation and vice! I was shocked. I believe I was so shocked that I didn't know what I was doing. I picked up the offending pillow . . .' The elderly voice trembled and stopped.

'Mr Dick,' said the Superintendent. 'Really . . .' He glanced helplessly at the lawyer, then: 'Take your time— I'll send for some coffee. Or would you prefer a glass of water?'

'Please, a drop of water, if it isn't too much trouble. This has all been such a shock to me—I believed I had closed it out of my mind, out of my mind.'

So much for Shields's opinion that it had been a cold, calculated murder. Chief Superintendent Wetherell listened to the rest of what Mr Dick had to say, then concluded the interview, switching off the tape and rewinding it so that a statement could be drafted for Dick's signature. The solicitor nodded gravely.

'I take it that my client can be released now, pending any further investigation of this unfortunate matter? My client has already been most generous with his information, and, may I remind you, in not laying an official complaint concerning the shameful manner in which he was brought here.'

He meant the handcuffs. Wetherell had apologized as

soon as he heard about that. 'It will take some time for a statement to be prepared,' he said.

Shields ought to be back by then.

In the end they had to come away without Tony Clifford, much to Jack Vernon's disgust. Shields was angry too, he would not allow Clifford or any other man to be above the law, but they were outnumbered. In addition Earl Kingston had guaranteed that Clifford would come to Clarence Square to sign a voluntary statement—concerning Crawford's presence on the estate the night Cal Frazer was killed.

Tomorrow, that was the guarantee. Clifford would come, with Trace and his uncle for support. Shields was banking on a coolness between Trace and his right-hand man now, once the poison about Clifford's betrayal of the Fleetway leaked out. In the meantime, Shields was going to have to talk to Alan Crawford.

'David?'

It was Billie Morgan, waiting in the shadows by the car. Shields signed for DC Vernon to go on while he stopped for a word. 'Billie? What's happened?' Her face was wet with tears.

'Leroy hasn't come home. We waited, it seemed like hours.'

Shields had no idea of the time, this had been a day that dragged on forever. He unlocked his car door, glad to see that Vernon had got a lift with the others. 'Get in, Billie,' he said.

It was twenty-five past nine. It didn't seem all that late for a teenager to be out, but the circumstances weren't normal.

'He's still on probation, David, and old Mrs Thomas is really strict with him. He has to be in before dark, without fail. He knows that.'

'Has she any idea where he might have gone?'

'He's taken to hanging around with Jed Monroe. She's not happy about it, but Leroy was so upset about Willis's death that she felt it would do him good to find another friend.'

Shields wondered if Monroe had made one of the gang around the recreation hall earlier. If he had, Shields hadn't seen him—he certainly hadn't seen Leroy there. But the trouble was, Leroy had seen Clifford at Workshop Street and Clifford was still free.

Shields couldn't help feeling defeated. After they had sweated blood to keep the peace in the face of the attack on Alan Crawford it would be ironic if they had to overturn the Fleetway in search of Leroy Thomas. Because of the rape complaint Shields had made a determined and painful effort to go by the book, to observe each niggling piece of protocol that might preserve the fragile status quo where the community was concerned. He didn't like it, but he had admitted, to himself at least, that Wetherell had the right to insist his policies were followed. The right because he had the responsibility when things went wrong.

It wouldn't be fair to ask Billie Morgan for any more help, he decided. But she must have read his mind.

'Do you want me to call at Jed's?'

'Could you? What would you say?'

'That Leroy's gran asked me to look out for him. They'd understand that. The Fleetway looks after its own, David. We might be able to prevent anything happening to him.'

'If word gets back to Trace? Yes, that might work. It's Clifford I'm afraid of. With word getting out of what he's been up to, he's bound to blame Leroy.'

'Leave it with me, then,' she persuaded, 'for tonight at least.'

Again the sense of defeat gripped Shields. There was

nothing else he could do. Without Crawford, without any support from his colleagues and with the almost open enmity of his superior, David Shields was feeling frustration as well as utter weariness.

'Try and get some sleep,' Billie said softly.

She didn't mean sleep. She was sitting close to him in the darkness, close enough for kissing. Her subtle perfume reached out to him, tentatively her hand touched his.

'You're very kind, Billie,' he said, his cold voice breaking the spell. 'I think I'll take your advice.' He hesitated. 'If you get any news of Leroy, though, you'll ring me? Whatever the time?'

'Of course.' She put her hand on the door handle, then turned back to him. 'If you keep on rejecting everything that's offered you, Chief Inspector, you're going to end up a very lonely man.'

'It depends on what's being offered,' he said evenly. 'Close the door.'

'Well?' Billie moved closer to him.

'You're feeling sorry for me, right? For making such a fool of myself?'

She was startled by the bitterness in his voice. The invincible Shields had never betrayed any lack of self-confidence before. 'I'd as soon feel sorry for a king cobra,' she declared roundly, holding his gaze. Then waited, sensing that he was on the brink of sharing his feelings. As he smiled she felt as if she had passed some sort of test, somehow made the right answer.

'I can't come to your flat,' he began.

'No. Anyway, I want to go round to see Mrs Monroe.'

'I could meet you somewhere, or—pick you up here? In an hour or so?' He touched her face gently. 'Or am I rushing you?' He smiled wryly as she made no reply. 'Some other time, perhaps.'

'No! That is, I mean, not some other time.' It would be too easy to lose him. 'I want you now. Tonight.' It wouldn't take her long to see Jed's mother and check if Leroy had been round. 'I'll be back within the hour.'

'Then I'll be waiting,' he promised.

'I tell you it was a complete balls-up—the whole thing. We catch one of those golliwogs taking a knife to a police officer —and what happens?' Detective-Constable Vernon wasn't waiting for an answer, just pausing for effect. 'Nothing. Stinking, rotten, bloody nothing!'

It was the following morning.

'At least the Sarge wasn't hurt,' ventured DC Mann.

'That's got fuck-all to do with it! Anyway, that Clifford might just as easily have skinned Crawford alive—and Mister bloody Shields would still have done nothing. Except go on kissing friend Kingston's arse!'

Kevin Mann made a show of getting a file out of his desk drawer. He wished Jack would shut up and that the others would go away. Hopwood in particular, who held similar views to Vernon, and didn't seem to care who heard them.

The two CID men had been in demand from the time they started the morning shift, the whole station was wild with rumour and they were the nearest available eye-witnesses. Mann had had to describe Sergeant Crawford's deplorable state, and tempers were high. Crawford had been granted sick leave but it was understood that the DCI had gone round to have a word with him.

'His own sergeant carved up like a dog's dinner and what does Shields do? Only arrest some bloody old age pensioner.'

'Had to call us in to do it, too,' said Hopwood. 'Even made Wilkes here cuff him to his wrist, like he was desperate or something.'

'He's losing his bottle, that's why.'

It wasn't really the guv'nor's fault, thought DC Mann, though he didn't care to voice his opinion. Not in present company. But it seemed to him that with the Weathercock breathing down his neck, Shields would have had to keep the lid on things.

'What about the old fellow?' he asked instead. 'Did he spend the night?'

Wilkes nodded. 'Shields rang Len Pickering about him. On no account was he to be let go. The Super didn't like it, you could tell. But with Shields being so busy keeping the peace, he must've felt he had to back him up.'

'Keeping the fucking peace,' Jack Vernon started on again. 'I'd like to keep the peace on the Fleetway—with a flamethrower!'

'Leave it, Jack.' Tim Wilkes got up to go. 'Shields has his orders just like we do.'

It wasn't orders that had taken David Shields round to the bedsit, not far from Clarence Square. The interlude with Billie Morgan had been just that—time out. After she had left the flat his problems had returned, intensified. A restless night hadn't improved Shields's state of mind, but of the many responsibilities weighing on him this was one of the most urgent.

'I'm sorry to come round so early,' he said, with unaccustomed politeness, 'but I thought you might have decided to go home and I wanted to talk to you first.'

'Come in, sir,' said Alan Crawford. 'I thought about it, going home I mean, but then—I don't want my mother to see me like this,' he said with a rush. In normal circumstances Alan Crawford was a good-looking young man. The savage hair-cutting had left him looking like a badly trimmed skinhead. Sticking plaster on the occasional cuts added to the bizarre effect.

'I understand.'

'It's a bit untidy . . .' He was referring to the state of his room.

'It doesn't matter.'

Nevertheless, Crawford started on a rapid clearing up, moving clothes off a chair so that the DCI could sit down. Putting the kettle on for a cup of coffee.

'Sit down, Alan.'

'I'll just rinse these cups, and then . . .'

'Sit down.' He was obeyed in silence. 'You know why I've come, don't you?'

Crawford brought his hand up to his non-existent hair in a pathetic action. 'I suppose I let you down,' he said slowly. 'Letting myself get trapped like that. Not knowing that Noah Franklyn wasn't to be trusted.'

'Noah has only one loyalty,' Shields said, 'and that's to the Fleetway. He helps us when it suits his purpose—I thought you understood that?'

'I—I suppose I never thought about it. But why did he trap me like that? He could've warned me that Clifford was slinking around.'

'I expect he wants Clifford out in the open and at odds with Trace Robertson.'

'If he'd told us what he knew . . .'

'He'd've ended up like Willis Charles.'

Crawford didn't like the silence, nor the way the guv'nor was regarding him. 'I made a mistake,' he said.

'Yes?' Shields wasn't going to help him this time.

'I knew I shouldn't have gone round to Cal's,' he burst out.

'No,' said Shields. 'So why did you?'

The guv'nor's steady politeness was unnerving. Usually by this time he would have anticipated Crawford's story, apology or whatever, called him a young fool and threatened dire penalties if he ever repeated the misdemeanour.

'I wanted to talk to her.' When the DCI didn't answer Crawford went on, 'I suppose I hoped she might change her story.' He had never seen Shields look so grim.

'What happened then?'

Crawford was shocked at the question. 'She was already dead! You've got to believe me, sir. God, it was awful.' He felt sick at the memory. 'You do believe me, don't you?'

'So what did you do?'

The Chief Inspector's face was calm, if a little pale, his voice unchanged. Crawford couldn't have picked the moment when he realized that the calm was determination, that Shields's pallor resulted from the effort of keeping his temper under control. He only knew he was suddenly afraid.

'I ran,' he confessed. 'I knew there'd be trouble if anyone saw me. Trouble with the estate, I mean.'

Shields didn't immediately comment, so Crawford got up to make the coffee. As he brought the cups to the table he said, 'I should've told you, I suppose.'

'Yes.' Shields bit the word off. He sat, looking at the coffee cup for a long moment, then got to his feet without touching it. Crawford thought he was going to leave without saying another word, but at the door Shields turned.

'If you want my advice,' he said slowly, 'you won't bother coming back to Clarence Square. It's nothing to do with your appearance, it's to do with something else. With what's inside. If we bring anyone to trial for Cal's murder you may be needed, but I hope not.'

'I know I've made you look bad . . .' Crawford began but got no further.

'Me? D'you think I care how any of us looks?' His voice held a note of incredulity. 'I deserve anything that happens because I was fool enough to think of lying for you. But do you think Cal's mother deserved what happened to her? I don't know how you coped with seeing Cal made into raw meat—it's given me nightmares. But you ran away and let her mother walk into that bedroom.' He had a lot more to say, Crawford sensed, but with a struggle he got control over himself. 'Clifford let you down lightly, Alan. I could wish he'd slit your throat while he was about it.'

CHAPTER 13

'I don't like it, David.'

'No, sir.' Chief Inspector Shields came back from the window to sit down again. The interview was taking place in Superintendent Wetherell's office. He had started to apologize for being late, but Wetherell was more concerned with the consequences of keeping Mr Dick locked up. Shields had intended to see the prisoner first but had been diverted by the Superintendent's urgent message.

'Have you talked to him?'

'Not since yesterday . . .'

'Well, he's confessed to killing Shipley—you know that, I suppose?'

'Yes, I half expected it. And, yes, I've seen the report. The man's a hypocrite.'

'What do you mean? Oh, keep still for goodness' sake!'

Restless as he was, Shields was finding it hard to sit and talk. 'Sorry. It's just that—look, sir, I was on my way to see him anyway but I need to know much more about what went on. After all, I found Shipley.' He paused, going back in his mind to the tidy flat. 'Dick didn't just kill him in anger, he put him to bed neatly and locked the door after himself. Then he went back to spreading sweetness and light to the benighted citizens.'

'Just because you don't like the man, that's no reason for appointing yourself judge and jury. It's an obvious case of dementia, Mr Dick will probably be found unfit to plead or there'll be a manslaughter verdict.'

'Not if I have anything to do with it!'

'There you go again.' Patiently, Wetherell lowered his voice and began to speak in persuasive, reasonable tones.

'David, think. You've been under a lot of strain, more than the rest of us, perhaps. You haven't had time to grasp the wider situation—politically, it's most unstable. We've got Councillor Kingston and his nephew coming in to make a statement. Then, hopefully, we'll have enough on those two young partners in crime to put a stop to the thieving that's been going on.'

'One of them killed Cal Frazer,' Shields reminded him.

'I admit it's logical, but we can't move without proof. Our top priority, David. If we're to clear this one it's got to be quickly! Now, at this point in time . . .'

Shields thought about it. Listening to Superintendent Wetherell's soothing platitudes helped, in a way. The monotonous voice quietened the tumultuous need to be everywhere at once and instead Shields picked up on the one thread that could unravel the whole complex issue.

If Cal had been speaking the truth, and he was sure she had, then it wasn't the whole truth. She had left something out, something so simple that they hadn't seen it. She had walked with Willis Charles to the Oldwall intersection and left him there, at about four-thirty on the Tuesday. The day of the riot. The day Shipley died.

There was a deep silence in the room as Wetherell came to the end of his peroration, but Shields was unaware of it. His mind was elsewhere. Willis couldn't have been on his way to see Shipley, in fact it was more likely that he had already seen him. Dick was lying about Shipley's perversion, he was sure. But why? Why had he mentioned Willis at all? Because he'd seen him—or because he himself had been seen?

'What is it?'

Striding around the room, Shields found himself explaining his theory to the Superintendent. 'It has to be the reason! Willis Charles hadn't done anything, it was what he'd seen that got him killed! It's in the post-mortem—head injuries, plural. That was what Cal left out of her story, it must have been.'

Wetherell had rarely seen anyone in such a state of controlled excitement. Shields was an irritating man who had a habitual air of superior knowledge and a trick of looking right through you when you were talking to him. Both must spring from this blind determination to see things through to the bitter end. An admirable quality that merely served to deepen Wetherell's conviction. He had to get rid of him, somehow. Wallsden was not the place to be ferreted through in search of inconvenient truths. Wallsden's priority was peace and harmony.

He must have been looking puzzled. Shields explained. 'She walked with him to the traffic lights, yes. But she wasn't the only one! Dick contacted somebody else, from Shipley's flat. He must've done, it's the only answer that fits! Somebody big enough and strong enough to walk with Willis and make sure he went where they wanted him to.' It would have been the house in Workshop Street, Shields thought. Willis Charles had been kept there, stunned, disoriented, already dying from the blow on the back of the head, ready to be taken outside when it was dark and added to the casualties of the riot. The overturned car had been a brilliant inspiration and he wondered which one of them had thought of it.

'Clarke,' he said suddenly.

'What about Clarke? You don't think he—'

'That's who Dick phoned.' Shields reconstructed the scene. The old man had been no problem—when he was eventually missed someone would break in and find he'd died in his sleep. But the youngster was a different matter and his body would have to be found. 'He must have sent somebody round to get Willis out of there—'

'No, no, no. All this is supposition, David. Are you

suggesting that Mr Dick, a frail, elderly man, hit Willis Charles on the head? What with? That flat was thoroughly checked, you know, thanks to your own efforts. Nothing there resembled a weapon.'

'No.'

Wetherell took a deep breath. 'So even if it did happen in the way you say, we still have nothing more to charge Mr Dick with. Willis Charles walked out of the Fleetway, walked, even if there was somebody supporting him. There's no case against Mr Dick.' Satisfied that Shields had no answer, Wetherell went on, 'Which leaves us with the murder of Miss Frazer as our top priority—a quick result on that would please everyone.'

'There's a message for you, sir.'

'Thanks, Kevin.' Shields picked up the slip of paper— Billie Morgan wanted him to phone her, urgently.

DC Mann carried on with his typing, thankful that Hoppy and Jack Vernon had finally taken themselves off somewhere. He'd ask about Alan as soon as the guv'nor was off the phone.

'Billie? What's happened? I thought everything was all right?' But it was bad news. 'Take it easy,' he urged. 'No one's blaming you.' He listened to her distraught voice admitting that she had been tricked the night before. Mrs Monroe had sworn it was a misunderstanding when she went round to see her again in the morning, no, she had seen nothing of Leroy—and Jed was out.

'We'll send somebody round to talk to her, and Mrs Thomas as well. If you could just . . .' He listened to her request. 'No,' he said at length. 'I'm sorry, Billie, I can't come yet. Kingston's on his way here . . .' She was worried of course, but Shields had other priorities. 'No way, I'm afraid. I've got to be here to talk to them. But if you'll stay with the old lady until someone gets there? . . . Yes, I know it's important. But I can't be in two places at once . . .' He was trying to be patient with her. 'As soon as I can. That's a promise. Thanks.'

Shields disconnected the call and contacted Sergeant Pickering on an inside line. Rapidly explaining the problem, he agreed that Wilkes and WPC Mason would be the people to send, for a start.

Only then did DC Mann get a chance to ask his question. 'Crawford? What about him?' Shields replied coldly.

'We were wondering how he was,' Mann said nervously, wishing he hadn't raised the subject. Shields's expression made it clear that he wanted nothing to do with his sergeant. It was a relief when the phone rang again.

'I'll be right down,' said Shields. It was the call he'd been waiting for.

Councillor Earl Kingston and the two younger men had been shown into the largest of the interview rooms, the one used earlier for the informal community meeting. Inspector Bidwell was already there, making polite conversation. PC Geoff Ellis was seated inconspicuously in the corner, in charge of the tape-recorder.

'I've just been telling Mr Kingston how much we appreciate his cooperation,' Bidwell told the DCI.

'This is a serious matter,' Councillor Kingston began. 'All the time the police were looking for one of our people they knew it was a white man who had visited that poor girl.' He motioned towards Tony Clifford. 'Clifford here saw him leave her, after ten o'clock at night. The same man, the very same, she had named as a police rapist.'

Good, thought Shields. 'Thank you, sir,' he said. 'I'll take Mr Clifford's statement now, if you and your nephew would like to go with the Inspector—'

Clifford's 'No way, man,' coincided with Kingston's more dignified objection. 'I came here, as I promised, to help with your inquiries, Mr Shields. But it is my duty to

see that the rights of our young brother are not infringed.'
It was no wonder he and the Superintendent got on like a
house on fire, thought Shields in exasperation. They spoke
the same language—pedantic tautology. Only their voices
differed, Wetherell's light and crisp, Kingston's dark and
rich.

While not precisely grinning, Tony Clifford had a complacent air about him that infuriated Shields. He stared at
the two gang members, not dissimilar in appearance and
attitude—there had to be some way to separate them and
get down to some serious interrogation. He decided to start
with the ostensible leader, Trace Robertson, and asked if
he had been with Clifford at the time.

He looked puzzled. 'I didn't have nothing to do with Cal
Frazer.'

'Where were you on Wednesday evening?'

'What is this? I told all this crap to you people in the
van. I told them, I didn't go nowhere near Cal's place.'

Shields looked quickly down at the transcripts he had
brought with him. 'You were at the hall talking to Noah
Franklyn . . .'

'Yeah, man. Noah and three, four other brothers. Talking
business.'

'It says here that the other brothers included your lieu-
tenant, Mr Clifford.'

'Yeah, that is—'

'You trying to trick us, man—'

'Really, Chief Inspector, I must—'

All three spoke at once, then stopped, one by one.

'Well?' Shields said into the sudden silence. 'Which of
you was lying?'

'You just trying to trick us,' Clifford repeated. 'Just trying
to protect your own man.'

'I'm not here to protect anybody,' said Shields, and
Jennifer Bidwell felt cold at his tones. Alan Crawford was

unforgiven and indeed, unforgivable. Then she saw the point of Shields's questioning—Clifford would either have to give up his own alibi or give up what he saw as the chance to get Sergeant Crawford into trouble.

He chose the former. His eyes narrowing, Clifford stated, 'Well, Trace must've made a mistake, that's all. Could happen to anybody.'

'Right,' breathed Shields. And then: 'It could indeed. Inspector, would you just take Trace through his statement again, just to correct the details? I'll carry on here. We don't want to waste too much of the councillor's time.'

It was as easy as that.

Jennifer Bidwell knew what to ask the gang leader, knew from Shields how to play on the sore point of Clifford's apparent alliance with the Fleetway's deadliest enemy. After Shields's harshness, her sympathetic approach was calculated to win Trace's confidence.

Shields struggled on, piece by piece, checking Clifford's story. At first he had to cope with Kingston's interruptions, but after a while the councillor became strangely silent. Clifford's tactic of verbal abuse was wasted on Shields's professionalism. In talking, Clifford talked too much.

'All right! But I never killed her—Cal's one of ours, the stupid slag.'

'But you know who did it,' pursued Shields relentlessly. 'You stood by and watched him, didn't you? Perhaps you even persuaded Cal to let you both in, introduced Chris to her as a friend?'

'No!' Clifford glared at him. 'No. She known Chris for a long time. Cal, she liked . . .' Shields could guess the rest.

'Whose idea was it that she cry rape?' Shields asked quietly. He'd known all along it had to be a set-up.

'What? Oh, that Cal she wanted to please the man, make some mischief for the filth. Chris, he din't like the way she done it.' Suddenly he swore. 'What about you talking at mister nice guy? I seen him sneak out Cal's flat.'

'You went in and saw what had happened?'

'No. I think Cal's still playing fucking games.'

'But you were there, and you're handy with a knife.' Then in an apparent change of mood Shields told Ellis to switch off the machine while they took a break. 'Perhaps our guests would appreciate some coffee?'

'You finished with us?' Clifford asked in disbelief. 'We can go?'

Shields temporized. 'Just let me make a quick phone call,' he suggested, making the internal connection. 'Sergeant Pickering? Ah, Len, I think we can go ahead and try for that warrant now. That's right, Chris Whittington on suspicion of the murder of Carolyn Frazer.' He looked across at Clifford. 'I think we have all the information we need. Mr Clifford's been most helpful.'

The subsequent outburst surpassed all Clifford's previous invective. Shields had heard all the words before but never in quite that sequence. Mr Kingston was shocked and demanded that it cease.

'I never told you nothing about whitey, you cunt, nothing! I never split—'

'On your mates?' Shields finished the sentence for him. 'So Whittington is your mate, then. That's what all this is about, isn't it? You two working together to stitch up the estate. Did Willis know? Or Cal Frazer? Did you ask Whittington to kill her for you, so that she couldn't say anything more to us?'

'No! Not that, it wasn't never—'

'Whose idea was it to cut her, yours? Or your partner's?'

Inspector Bidwell thanked Trace Robertson for his information. She felt sorry for him now, sorry for the haunted look gradually replacing his anger.

She was sure he had not known of the scam that Clifford and Whittington were working, but it had become obvious as he answered her questions that he had been made to look a complete fool.

'It isn't over yet,' she said. 'Some of your people might get the wrong idea—we'll have to charge your friend Clifford.'

'They'll do what me and Noah tell them,' Trace said with a touch of his old bravado. 'My uncle'n' all, now he know what Cliff been up to.'

Just then a weary-looking Shields came into the room. Bidwell asked him if Trace could rejoin his uncle. 'He's told us everything he knows, I'm sure,' she said.

Shields nodded. 'We've decided to book Clifford on conspiracy to commit murder—we're just going to get Whittington.'

'You'll take care?'

'I'm taking half the uniforms in the station, as well as Jack Vernon.' He paused as if wanting to say something more.

'Can I help?'

Shields nodded. 'I'm worried about the situation on the Fleetway. You know Leroy Thomas is missing? Billie Morgan has agreed to stay with his grandmother, but I'd be glad if you could go back there with Trace and Councillor Kingston. You could liaise with the councillor about setting up a house to house search . . .'

'Yes, of course. Come along, Trace. We'll get a car organized.'

'Jen.' Shields hadn't finished. 'Take Len Pickering with you, this time.'

Bidwell smiled to herself, remembering how David Shields had rescued her on a previous occasion. Then she remembered what had happened to Sergeant Crawford. There was nothing to smile about.

*

DC Vernon was driving the CID contingent for a change and feeling pleased with what looked like the possibility of promotion. There was a vacancy for acting-sergeant, at least until Crawford came back. If he didn't come back, well, that was even better. He settled himself more comfortably into the driving seat. Action at last! He was looking forward to it, there'd been enough pussy-footing around.

The car following was under the command of Inspector Powell and they had a vanload of reinforcements as well. Shields must be taking this one seriously. Vernon thought it typical that they could turn out a show of force for one white toerag like Whittington but weren't allowed to move in on the mass disorder of the Fleetway at all.

Mid-afternoon. Not the best time to catch a villain at home, but Whittington was already under warning, it seemed. Would he run, or would he fight? The odds were on running in a situation like this, but it was hard to know, the political complications could affect Whittington's decision—Whittington senior might be looking forward to a day in court.

His thoughts were interrupted by the radio coming to life with a message for the DCI.

'Shields here. What's the problem?'

'An emergency, I'm afraid. I've just had a call from control—they want us diverted to the Fleetway. Tim Wilkes has reported a riot situation. We're to get our people out —I've already sent the van.'

'Good man.' God, Jennifer Bidwell was there, too. Why was he always in the wrong place! He should have gone with her, left Whittington to . . .

'I think we should go as well,' Powell was saying.

'Yes, of course. Good luck.' Shields closed the transmission, telling the others what had happened.

Disappointed, Vernon waited for instructions. When none came, he started to pull out into the right-hand lane.

'What are you doing?'

'I'm going to make a turn—we can cut through—'

'No. We're picking up Whittington.'

'Three of us?' There would be three men to face if the elder brother was at home. It didn't look nearly so much like fun, now.

It wasn't.

Vernon was sent round the back of the respectable semi-detached house to cut off the retreat, while Shields and Kevin Mann approached the front door. It was answered by Robert Whittington himself, looking wary.

'I've nothing more to say to you, Mr Shields.'

'It's really Chris we'd like a word with, this time.'

'Why? You've already said your piece. What's this all about?'

'Is he in?'

'What d'you want with him?'

Shields heard a noise in the kitchen at the back of the house. 'Is your son in, Mr Whittington? We need to talk to him.' Without touching the older man, Shields pushed past him and raced through in time to see the back door closing. On the other side Chris Whittington was trying to turn the key in the lock and there ensued a kind of tug of war before he abandoned it and took to his heels across the back yard.

The walled garden was mostly devoted to vegetables, with the occasional miniature fruit tree. DC Vernon was guarding the gate that led out to the small park beyond. Whittington backed up against a garden shed, then, as the two officers approached, he whipped out his knife.

It was a long, narrow, double-sided weapon. Shields found himself taking a mental note as if this were a training exercise. He felt he could describe it down to the finest detail. If this had been an exercise situation the next thing, doubtless, would be to wait for reinforcements? They could certainly do with them.

'Is that the knife you used on Cal Frazer?' Shields asked in an almost conversational tone. He approached Whittington slowly, calmly, not daring to take his eyes off the knife, hoping Vernon wouldn't do anything unexpected to distract either of them.

Whittington made a few crude passes in the air. The knife was razor sharp and he looked very much at home with it. 'You want it, you can come and get it.'

Shields ignored the taunt. 'It would be better for you if you just handed that thing over,' he began.

'Oh, you can have it, copper. You can have it right up your arse. Or—' swiftly he changed it from hand to hand as if to demonstrate his mastery—'I could start with your long nose—teach you to keep it out of other people's business.'

'Keep back, Vernon,' Shields warned his colleague quickly, without shifting his gaze. 'I'll take this one on my own.'

It was a textbook situation. They had practised this sort of thing often enough—Shields just hoped the DC had his wits about him. 'I've got all the time in the world, Chris,' he said quietly.

Whittington laughed, a high-pitched and panicky sound. He didn't like the way the other copper had backed off, he couldn't watch them both now. The knife felt slippery in his hand as he sweated, tension mounting. He was going to have to do it! Half horrified, half exhilarated at the prospect of sinking the precious steel into living flesh, he made a lunge, a wild sweep at Shields's face, and laughed again as the man instinctively flinched away.

'Come on, little piggy,' he screamed. 'Come and get your fucking throat cut!' Any fear of retribution had left Whittington now, he was on a natural high at the thought of inflicting pain. He had been too quick with the black girl, he reasoned, not realizing what a kick he could have got from slicing through live meat. 'Come on, come and get your—'

The bastard, oh, the bastard! Whittington sensed the alien presence behind him now, creeping up, grabbing at his arm. Both of them now, a grip like steel on his wrist as he struggled madly to do some harm. Twisting and turning, he lashed out, managing to take the knife into his free left hand for a few seconds. He'd show them! Blood was what he wanted now, blood to make their hands slippery, blood to scare them away from him. The knife was an extension of his nerve-endings. The knife was his mouth and he was going to drink blood.

CHAPTER 14

DC Mann's reputation was for dependability—he was the sort of officer who could be counted on to obey orders to the letter. Initiative, though, was something else again.

He looked helplessly at Robert Whittington, then followed him into the kitchen. 'I'm sorry, sir, you can't go out there,' he said, firmly enough, as Whittington put his hand on the doorknob.

'I want to know what's happening. I demand to know —I've got my rights.'

'Yes, sir. I'll have a word with the Chief Inspector when he gets back.'

There was confused shouting from outside.

'Why don't you sit down, sir. Or would you like a cup of tea?'

'Don't treat me like an elderly imbecile! I'm an Englishman and this is my home. That still means something, even in these degenerate days . . .'

'Yes, sir.' In the silence Mann stared around at the neatly appointed kitchen and wondered where Mrs Whittington was. There was no way three men living alone would keep a place so tidy. 'Er,' he began.

'Well? What is it now?'

Before he could ask Whittington about his wife there was a noise from outside, Vernon's voice, high-pitched and frantic. 'Kevin, for Christ's sake open the door!'

'Cold water—' Shields was behind him—'and something to use for bandages. But you'd better call an ambulance first.'

It was like something out of a horror movie, both men

liberally splattered with blood and dragging between them an inanimate and bloodied figure.

Robert Whittington made a spluttering noise and swayed.

'Catch him, Kevin!'

He was unconscious as Mann folded him into a chair and draped him forward across the kitchen table.

There were clean teacloths in the drawer. DC Mann made the call for assistance, then helped Shields to make a tourniquet around Chris Whittington's arm.

'Get a plastic bag, will you, Kevin—the knife's outside where he dropped it,' said Shields breathlessly. 'It's the one he used on Cal Frazer.' He looked round the kitchen, which was beginning to look like a World War I dressing station.

'Are you all right?' Shields was talking to Jack Vernon, who was using one of the towels on his own hand.

'I'll get that little bleeder for this,' rasped Vernon savagely. He had a deep cut on his right hand and others that stung like mad.

Most of the blood shed had been Whittington's, who by accident or design had slashed at his own wrists when it became clear that he couldn't fight his way out. He had taken little interest in the subsequent proceedings.

He surfaced briefly, sick and dizzy. There was light-headedness and a strange feeling of not belonging to his body. As the dizziness passed, Chris Whittington found himself sitting at the kitchen table, being watched by the sneaky copper who'd got him from behind. The other one was doing something to his dad.

He squealed, 'You've killed him! You've killed my dad!'

That was when the ambulance arrived.

Driving himself back to Clarence Square, Kevin Mann felt like the sole survivor of a battlefield. Besides the inanimate

Whittingtons, father and son, the ambulance had taken the other two detectives in as passengers. Jack Vernon, still complaining bitterly, was obviously going to need stitches. Mann thought it likely that the guv'nor would need treatment as well. It had been a shambles.

'A bit of a shambles, Sarge,' he found himself repeating to the duty sergeant who was covering for Len Pickering.

'Can't do anything about it at the moment,' said the sergeant, picking up the phone to relay the news to Superintendent Wetherell. 'Everybody's up at the estate. You'd better—Sir? Yes, DC Mann's here, sir, the others have gone to the hospital. Yes, apparently they tried to arrest Whittington and he pulled a knife.' He listened attentively. 'That's what I thought, sir.' He turned his attention back to the DC. 'You can get yourself a cup of tea first. Start writing your report and the Super'll send for you when he's got time.' Other things were more important, it seemed.

In the canteen DC Mann found an off-duty collator and tried to get some information out of him. For a start, where was everybody?

'Where've you been all day?'

Kevin Mann mightn't be the most forceful occupant of the CID room, but he knew better than to take cheek from back-room staff. 'We've just picked up a killer—with a knife.'

The other looked unimpressed. 'Oh yes?' He peered closely at Mann's jacket. 'There's a spot of blood on your sleeve,' he said.

'Never mind that—what's happening at the Fleetway?' He had just remembered Inspector Powell's diversion, how what should have been their back-up had found something better to do.

'The usual thing. Some old lady had a seizure and the mob blamed it on the constable interrogating her. By the time the reinforcements got there it had turned into a stand-off.'

'What happened?'

'Dunno. Last I heard they were negotiating to let the ambulance through. Trouble is . . .'

'What?' Mann put his cup down heavily, so that some of the nearly cold tea slopped around. 'What else?' No wonder the Weathercock hadn't got time to see him.

'One of the stringers must've been hanging around and phoned his paper, early on. The whole media's there by now, TV cameras included. This one's going to hit the six o'clock news. Live.'

Back in his office, Superintendent Wetherell had already been given the same information. He had made a brief visit to the scene earlier but had left, aware that there was nothing more he could do. He had spoken to one of the reporters, playing down—as far as was possible—the situation. But he couldn't afford to stretch their credulity too far. He stressed the fact that the constable conducting the inquiry —no, of course it wasn't an interrogation—had been a mature and sensible man, and had had a WPC with him.

What he wanted was Shields. It wasn't a matter of a scapegoat, he reasoned, it was a matter of setting things straight. It was Shields who had ordered Tim Wilkes and WPC Mason into the danger zone and then compounded things by sending Inspector Bidwell after them.

Fortunately, Jennifer Bidwell was quite safe.

She was standing at the window in Ron Purvis's flat, watching the scene outside.

'Where's Mr Shields, then?' Ron asked again.

She didn't know, any more than she knew where Len Pickering was—Len had suggested she start by making inquiries in Victor House, where there were people who were known to be friendly.

She had been watching a brief skirmish—one of the

cameramen had got too close to the crowd that surrounded the block and had to be rescued by a uniformed policeman.

It would be dark soon.

'Might as well have the telly on,' said Ron philosophically. 'Come and sit down, my dear. There's nothing else you can do, is there? We may as well see what's happening.'

Bidwell's instructions had been to stay where she was, pending a resolution of the situation. It made sense, she supposed though she would rather have been active. It was a weird, disorienting experience to sit in the middle of the situation that was being described in flamboyant terms, to sit safely watching one's own part in it.

'An unfortunate misunderstanding.' Superintendent Wetherell, the master of the understatement, was being interviewed. From the way he spoke, the police presence was merely to protect property and to protect the misguided citizens against their own excesses. He advocated patience. He also expressed a guarded wish that the news media could have found something better to do.

That was when the studio chose to switch from the videotaped interview to action at the scene. Jennifer got a rather better view of the incident she had already witnessed from the window, of the cameraman being hassled. Unfortunately, they unaccountably missed the police part in the rescue.

And then they were live, with a brave reporter raising his voice above the chanting of the crowd. He spoke movingly of the unfortunate grandmother of a young man the police were keen to interview, how her distress at his absence had been heightened by the insensitive questioning she had been subjected to. The reporter managed to infer that Mrs Thomas was frail, elderly, and that Constable Wilkes was nearly six foot tall and brutal with it. He spoke of Leroy, young and—he didn't actually mention intellectual handicap, but his words were meant to leave that impression—and on the run from the police. It was not known what crime he might have committed but it was thought to be breach of probation. Again the subtle suggestion that the police presence was there to find Leroy and that was why the estate was up in arms.

Before the bulletin switched to other topics there was a studio announcement that they would be monitoring progress, throughout the night if need be.

Inspector Bidwell leaned forward to switch the set off, needing to take stock of the situation, and nearly missed the next item. 'After this break we take you to our reporter at Wallsden General Hospital, where a man has just died after being taken into police custody.'

They wouldn't let him talk to him.

Obstinately Shields stayed where he was, determined to see Whittington, if only for a few minutes. Jack Vernon had been treated and sent home, Shields had had his own cuts seen to but still he refused to leave.

'I'm sorry, Chief Inspector, but these men are dangerously ill. Even if they were conscious, I couldn't allow you to speak to either of them.'

Robert Whittington, it seemed, had had a heart attack. Shields felt sorry about that, but couldn't see that he could have done things differently. Except by not arresting the younger Whittington at all.

Again his mind went back to the scene in the garden. They had bungled it between them, he knew. When Vernon had crept up behind Whittington he should have hit him over the head rather than grabbing for the knife—but that was to be wise after the event. It wasn't policy to attack the person they were trying to arrest. But that knife had been murderously sharp—he looked down at his bandaged hands.

Waiting was one of the things that Shields wasn't very

good at, but like every other facet of the job, when it had to be done he could do it. He walked along the corridor in search of a telephone, but the only one he saw was already in use. He went back to the waiting-room.

His brain, unlike his body, was unable to rest. The facts and fictions of the case, or cases, went whirling round his mind and he grasped at one and then another. Had his hands been free he would have attempted to make notes but as it was he was forced to sit still. He should have been resting but instead he continued to worry his way through the events of the past two weeks.

'Chief Inspector.' A loud and disapproving voice brought him back to awareness.

'Yes?' He got to his feet quickly but couldn't shake himself awake. As if in a dream, or nightmare, he heard the doctor tell him that his prisoner had died without recovering consciousness.

'Died?' This couldn't be happening. 'Are you sure?' Shields asked the inane question without thinking.

'There has been no mistake on our part, Chief Inspector. We did everything possible but unfortunately he had lost too much blood. And since there is no question of your seeing his father I suggest that you are now free to leave.'

'Of course.' Shields felt suddenly sick. He hadn't killed Chris Whittington but he had inadvertently been the cause of his death. Now they could never know for certain what part he had played in the Fleetway murders. In a sense Tony Clifford was off the hook now, he could lay as much blame as he liked on his late partner.

At the door to the waiting-room Shields was told by a businesslike nurse that there was someone to see him and, assuming it was a colleague from Clarence Square, Shields went with her.

There were several people in the room, but Shields only registered one, the one who thrust a microphone into his face. 'Can you tell us what happened, Mr Shields? This man who died in police custody, did he have anything to do with the riot on the Fleetway estate?' Suddenly they were all asking questions. Was he aware that his suspect's father had had a heart attack? Had he been able to question his victim again before he died? Was it true that an elderly pensioner had been arrested? What was it all about?

When finally Shields began to speak they were silent for the few seconds it took them to hear the words, 'No comment.' After that the babble broke out all over again. There was a TV camera in the room now, and seemingly no chance of escape.

'I have nothing to say—I have no comment to make.' His words twisted themselves fantastically inside his head. Someone was referring to the blood on his hands. He heard the next question as 'Have you anything to say before sentence is passed?'

Minutes later he was being escorted down a flight of steps, a warder on either side. The businesslike nurse was back, and with her the disapproving doctor. Together they had separated Shields from the baying pack and he found himself flat on his back in one of the casualty cubicles.

'We may as well change that dressing while you are here,' the doctor was saying. 'But really, you should have gone home when we told you to.'

Shields couldn't argue with that.

Cold and clammy, the hesitant light of early morning was infiltrating the Fleetway estate. It found nothing in the deserted passageways but litter.

There was nobody about. The police contingent had sensibly retreated as they noted a gradual lessening of the forces arrayed against them. The residents, feeling the cold, had one by one found better things to do than maintain an aggressive posture. Here and there, small voices of reason had urged a rethink—to be made from the comfortable normality of home. Earl Kingston was one such small voice. Billie Morgan was another.

Billie had spent the early part of the evening in Mrs Thomas's flat, waiting with her for the ambulance. She had taken Anita Mason's place at the old lady's bedside, reassuring her, saying with a confidence she didn't feel that Leroy was bound to be back soon.

Afterwards she had joined Noah and one or two others in spreading a little subversive sweet reason. The difference was that while Noah was circulating among the activists, Billie confined her attention to the angry-eyed women whose struggles for a decent if inadequate living were being hindered by the disturbance. As a result, those men returning to their wives for encouragement and hot food were being persuaded to give up and go to bed.

Now, at first light, she was going home.

Billie Morgan wasn't just tired, she was at that stage, just past exhaustion, when every routine action demanded mental as well as physical effort. She was even past her anger with David Shields, having looked out for him time after time until unbelievingly realizing that he wasn't coming.

She had earlier seen and spoken to Inspector Bidwell, who had drawn certain conclusions. But even David's defection didn't matter any more—he was just one more louse who'd let her down. It was the effect of his absence on the Fleetway situation that seemed more real than any personal sense of loss. Her only tears came when she discovered that the lift in Nelson House still wasn't working and she had to drag her rebellious body up six flights of stairs.

Opening her door to find there had been an obvious intruder in the kitchen annoyed her, but didn't shock her into proper awareness. It was only the collision with a large male body in the dimness of her bedroom that did that.

'With all due respect,' Shields had begun, wearily.

'Respect? That's an odd word for you to use.'

Shields found he could remember every word, every nuance, of the previous evening's interview.

Chief Inspector Shields had left the hospital late on Friday night, but instead of going straight home, had returned to Clarence Square. There he had been brought face to face with Superintendent Wetherell's despairing anger. Wetherell could be calm in most situations, but publicity as bad as this was the exception. Shields was put in the distinctly unusual position of having to listen and not answer back.

'I believe I gave you instructions—right at the start of this situation—not to stir things up! But did you listen?'

'But . . .'

'No! You went ahead on this—this wild goose chase! Determined we were faced with a murder situation, you poked about until it became one. All these deaths are down to your intervention, Shields. All monuments to your— what was it driving you? Ambition? Pride?' The Superintendent had gone on, at some length.

In the cold light of early morning, it was hard for Shields to believe that he had said nothing, just sat and taken it without attempting to defend his actions.

He glanced at the watch he was still wearing, in common with most of his clothes. It had been Len Pickering, he remembered, who had found him asleep over the table in the canteen, a cup of cold tea beside him. Len who had found him the unofficial bed and guided him to it. Shields swung his feet to the floor and scratched at his chin. Len would know where there was a shaver he could use.

His thoughts went back to the Superintendent's accusations. Logically, they were well founded, he supposed. If he had let things be, the Fleetway might have remained calm—and that was Wetherell's yardstick for police procedure.

There had been more to do last night than argue with Superintendent Wetherell. Shields had already dictated a preliminary report on the death of Chris Whittington, checked that the Fleetway situation didn't need him. There was no question now of extending the search for Leroy Thomas.

'You've heard what the damned reporters are saying?' Wetherell had demanded. 'That we're persecuting that boy, looking for him because of some parole infringement! That's your doing, too.'

'I felt that Leroy was in danger . . .'

'Danger? On the Fleetway? For your information, every unemployed juvenile on that estate is in danger. And what about young Whittington? He's dead, Shields, dead! You don't seem to realize what that means.'

It meant a heyday for every police-baiting reporter, Shields was well aware of that. But still his priorities weren't Wetherell's.

Eventually Wetherell had given up and gone home, but Shields had been beyond such common sense.

Now after a shower and a clumsy shave, David Shields went up to his own office. It was too early for there to be many people about and he was glad of that. He supposed things had been as bad as this before, but he couldn't think of the occasion. His instincts were to get out, to put this manor, his whole career perhaps, behind him. But first there was the paperwork to get straight.

He felt he knew now what had happened, why Willis Charles had been killed. He thought again about the slippery Mr Dick, who would probably never be charged with the second, unforgivable, murder. Chris Whittington was beyond justice too. Shields's hands were sore—getting the bandages wet hadn't helped. He wondered how soon he could wake Tony Clifford for the interview that had been postponed last night.

Just then the phone rang.

It was a strangely excited Billie Morgan. 'I rang you at home, over and over. Whatever time d'you start work?'

'What is it, Billie? What's happened, are you all right?'

It was the best news they had had in a long while, the only good news of the entire investigation. 'I've just given him some breakfast, poor kid, I don't think he'd had anything to eat for ages. We were right about him being missing, Cliff had locked him in one of the empty flats but he'd managed to make his way out when nobody came back for him. He was afraid to stay at his gran's place without her, so he broke into mine, the little sod. All the same, he's all right, David, Leroy's safe!'

CHAPTER 15

In the event, the news that Whittington was dead had a placating effect on the Fleetway estate. That he had died by his own knife struck the residents as natural justice—and for once the police had not obstructed its course. Poor Cal Frazer was avenged.

Even the press had difficulty sustaining their accusations of police brutality when the facts about Whittington's death became known. Once he was identified as the murderer of Cal Frazer, he changed from innocent victim to crazed slasher—and how many more such killers walked the streets of Wallsden, waiting to strike? What were the police doing about it?

Tony Clifford's testimony was enough to convict the deceased Whittington, over and over again. As Shields had foreseen, Cliff happily blamed Chris Whittington for everything from the original concept of the thefts to the decision to silence Cal. 'Man, he was murder with that knife.'

To Shields's private satisfaction, Clifford was able to explain away the complexities of Willis Charles's death—he had become extraordinarily helpful now that he had nothing to lose.

It was as Shields had thought. Horace Clarke was involved at the outset. 'Like he got this call to go round to old Shipley's place—only he's run into the brothers working High Street instead. Left his shiny motor behind and come round to me and Chris at headquarters.' The Workshop Street house, where Clarke had arrived in a panic, menaced by the crowds on the street and in a state because of the threatening phone call. 'Man, he so scared he just about shit hisself.'

'Did he tell you what the call had been about?'

'Nah. Only how somebody got to go round the Fleetway, urgent like.'

'And it was you who went?' Shields deliberately kept his tone non-committal, interested not in making accusations but in recording the boring facts.

'That old fool,' Clifford began. 'He's only hit Willis over the head with his stick. Now he's panic time. Only the man—' he meant Clarke—'tells me this Dick-head, he knows what's going on. Means we got to do what he say.'

'And that was?'

'To get Willis out, anyplace, and forget we ever been there.'

'Did he say how Willis came to be in Shipley's flat?' Shields asked, trying to tie up loose ends.

'He's run errands for Shipley and them old folks. Old Dick-head, he was mad at him, seems he come out of the kitchen when the man didn't know he was in the place at all. He said he was to take him away and shut him up.'

'We? You and who else?'

'That Cal, of course. My poor Cal Frazer, she into everything up to her pretty neck. Willis, he's sitting up and looking sick when we arrive—he come with us quiet as a lamb.'

Clifford confirmed that he had taken Willis Charles to Workshop Street, where they had learned from Clarke that his car had been overturned. 'He swear some, then he clear out saying he was never there.' They waited till dark, then carried Willis to the scene, strapped him in the front seat of the Renault and turned the car on its back. 'Chris, he thought that some joke, to use the man's own motor.'

Clifford was going to give evidence against Mr Dick when the latter came to trial. He would give evidence against Iggy Sparrow as well—all he wanted in return was protection from Sparrow's reprisals. After all, he himself had done nothing against the law, only a little harmless thieving. 'You not going to charge me for cutting the hair on that fuzz?'

No, there would be no charge arising from the assault on Detective-Sergeant Crawford. Clarence Square couldn't afford the details of Alan's behaviour to come out. Shields had written a clear and damning report, intending to recommend his sergeant's summary dismissal. He was strongly tempted to write his own resignation to go with it, feeling, as he still did, a sense of responsibility.

It was that sense of responsibility that led Shields to redraft his report on Crawford, in the end. To cut short a career that had been, until this point, so promising, went against the grain. Sergeant Crawford's moral failure was a one-time thing that would probably never be repeated and the man deserved a second chance, Shields supposed. Just so that he never had to work alongside him again.

The arrest of Iggy Sparrow and his minders went remarkably smoothly, Iggy being quite used to arrest and expecting to walk straight out of the station again. But he hadn't reckoned on Tony Clifford as a source of police information and this time they picked up the goods as well.

By then Billie Morgan had brought Leroy in for a quiet talk with Chief Inspector Shields, who spent the rest of the weekend happily filling in the gaps.

Even Superintendent Wetherell was in a reasonably happy mood next time Shields saw him. Wallsden's troubles were no longer news—a rumour that a royal duke was paying child maintenance to a member of the palace's domestic staff had taken over from riot as the significant headline of the day.

The Fleetway estate was calm enough now, its usual

simmering calm, with the suppressed threat of trouble to come. Councillor Earl Kingston had professed shock and dismay at the ultimate source of his community funding, although it was hard to believe that he was as innocent as he appeared. But with fraud, burglary and conspiracy inextricably mixed with murder the court case was going to take some putting together. In the meantime relations with the Fleetway would have to be kept sweet and that meant believing everything Kingston told them.

The Superintendent, while not going so far as to apologize for his intemperate language, was able to admit that Shields had done a good job, within limits.

'Whittington is out of circulation, which makes the manor that much safer,' he said. 'Though it's a pity you couldn't have brought him in alive. It always looks bad when a prisoner dies in custody, it reflects on all of us. Finding that other boy safe and well made up for the bad handling of the situation on the Fleetway, I feel.' Wetherell paused, as if waiting for some reaction from the Chief Inspector. 'Don't you agree?'

'I'm glad Leroy Thomas is safe—he's also been very helpful to us.' Shields still felt guilty about taking a risk with the boy's life, but he wasn't about to make any confessions to the Superintendent. There was one topic he felt obliged to raise, though.

'You've had a chance to look at my report? On Sergeant Crawford,' he queried.

Wetherell frowned. 'A nasty business. I would have said he had the makings of an excellent officer—he modelled himself on you, you know.'

'I'm sorry.'

The two men sat in silence, looking at each other, neither one of them liking what they saw. Loyalty to his men was very high on Wetherell's list of personal priorities. He saw

Shields's criticism of Crawford as a self-righteous attempt to dissociate himself from failure. 'You've done what you thought best, I've no doubt. I'll see that your report is acted on.'

'He'll be demoted?'

'And transferred. Yes.'

'I understand. Is that all, sir? Because . . .'

'Sit down, David. There's something else I want to discuss with you.'

Discuss, thought Shields. That meant another lecture on the good of the community and the social responsibility of an informed police force. He'd heard it all before, how minimum interference in the Fleetway's affairs would have prevented the recent headlines vilifying Clarence Square. He thought about the mistakes he had made, but knew that he had made no mistake in determining to investigate the death of Willis Charles.

Then he realized that Wetherell's talk was heading in a different direction.

'. . . characteristics that, important as they are, are largely wasted in a team situation such as we have here in Wallsden.' Shields felt himself looking blank as the Superintendent continued: 'You have an independence of mind, David, a personal integrity that makes it hard for you to compromise with the pragmatism of community work.' As always, Superintendent Wetherell looked pleased with the sound of his own voice, while Shields worked hard to find the meaning behind the eloquence.

'You're suggesting I should apply for a transfer at the same time, sir?'

'Ah. I wouldn't put it in quite those terms, David. As I think I mentioned before, you have to think of your career. Just a transfer, no. We'll have to do better than that.'

So what was the devious bastard suggesting?

'I think you should be looking for promotion. An independent command would suit you, wouldn't it? Make use of those sterling qualities I just mentioned. In fact—' Wetherell made a quick search through a stack of papers —'I noticed this the other day. Right up your street, I'd have thought.'

'Yes, sir?'

'Of course, it would mean your leaving the Met, but the rank of superintendent should make up for that, I feel. I'd certainly be willing to put in a good word for you.' The Chief Superintendent smiled briefly to indicate his willingness to recommend Shields to somebody—anybody—who would take him off Wallsden's hands. 'Give yourself some time to think about it, David. Not too long, of course—they might find someone else to fill the vacancy. I'm sure we can plod on with any prosecutions after all your brilliant work, so don't let that side of it worry you.'

How very thoughtful, Shields mused as he studied the information. Sole charge in the back of beyond—there was something tempting about it. To be a big frog in a smallish pond had its attractions, especially considering that he would be out of reach of Superintendent Wetherell's interference. Promotion was important too.

'So when's the do?'

'You mean for the DCI?' Sergeant Pickering pulled a face. 'You'd better ask the Super, Hoppy,' he said.

'Only I thought, if we want the Ring o'Bells we might need to get on to it smartish.' Constable Hopwood took a personal interest in the drinking timetable. 'They've other commitments this time of year. You could have a word with Biddy?'

Len Pickering shook his head. 'No. It was Mr Wetherell

that dropped me the hint, he'll be the one to know what's what.'

The Chief Superintendent was in an expansive state of mind when Len dropped in on him later. He had roughed out a first class reference for David Shields and was rather pleased with his magnanimity. He gave Pickering an overview of the new position, in so far as he saw it.

'It sounds very interesting,' Len said tactfully.

He said as much to Chief Inspector Shields later on in the afternoon, finding him alone in the CID office. 'You'll find it a bit different, though, won't you? I mean, there's always plenty going on in Wallsden.'

Shields stared at the Sergeant as if he didn't know what he was talking about.

'I'm sorry if it's still confidential,' Len went on awkwardly, 'but some of the boys want to get the do organized —any excuse for a booze-up.'

'In that case,' said Shields quietly, 'by all means go ahead and organize one. I'm sure somebody will be able to think of an excuse.'

Pickering swallowed a smart answer and began, 'Er, the Super mentioned . . .'

Shields smiled. It didn't make Len Pickering feel any better.

'Let me guess,' suggested Shields. 'Wetherell said that he had recommended my promotion on the grounds of my superior abilities?'

'Something like that, sir.'

'In spite of appearances—' Shields interrupted himself to invite Sergeant Pickering to sit down and make himself comfortable. Then he went on, 'In spite of his benign exterior, our Super is a very devious man.' He looked at Pickering for a long moment. 'I'm not telling you anything you don't know,' he said flatly.

Pickering grinned. 'Not really.' But he's obviously not

as devious as some buggers, not excepting the one within spitting distance. 'So Wallsden won't be looking for a new DCI, after all? I'd say that's good news.'

'Thanks. Give Hopwood my apologies—about his party.' Shields glanced at his watch. 'But if you're free later, I might buy you a drink.'

L